Jimbo

Jimbo

A Fantasy

Algernon Blackwood

MINT EDITIONS

Jimbo: A Fantasy was first published in 1909.

This edition published by Mint Editions 2021.

ISBN 9781513283111 | E-ISBN 9781513288130

Published by Mint Editions®

 **MINT
EDITIONS**

minteditionbooks.com

Publishing Director: Jennifer Newens
Design & Production: Rachel Lopez Metzger
Project Manager: Micaela Clark
Typesetting: Westchester Publishing Services

Contents

I

"Rabbits"

Jimbo's governess ought to have known better—but she didn't. If she had, Jimbo would never have met with the adventures that subsequently came to him. Thus, in a roundabout sort of way, the child ought to have been thankful to the governess; and perhaps, in a roundabout sort of way, he was. But that comes at the far end of the story, and is doubtful at best; and in the meanwhile the child had gone through his suffering, and the governess had in some measure expiated her fault; so that at this stage it is only necessary to note that the whole business began because the Empty House happened to be really an Empty House—not the one Jimbo's family lived in, but another of which more will be known in due course.

Jimbo's father was a retired Colonel, who had married late in life, and now lived all the year round in the country; and Jimbo was the youngest child but one. The Colonel, lean in body as he was sincere in mind, an excellent soldier but a poor diplomatist, loved dogs, horses, guns and riding-whips. He also really understood them. His neighbours, had they been asked, would have called him hard-headed, and so far as a soft-hearted man may deserve the title, he probably was. He rode two horses a day to hounds with the best of them, and the stiffer the country the better he liked it. Besides his guns, dogs and horses, he was also very fond of his children. It was his hobby that he understood them far better than his wife did, or than any one else did, for that matter. The proper evolution of their differing temperaments had no difficulties for him. The delicate problems of child-nature, which defy solution by nine parents out of ten, ceased to exist the moment he spread out his muscular hand in a favourite omnipotent gesture and uttered some extraordinarily foolish generality in that thunderous, good-natured voice of his. The difficulty for himself vanished when he ended up with the words, "Leave that to me, my dear; believe me, I know best!" But for all else concerned, and especially for the child under discussion, this was when the difficulty really began.

Since, however, the Colonel, after this chapter, mounts his best hunter and disappears over a high hedge into space so far as our story is concerned, any further delineation of his wholesome but very ordinary type is unnecessary.

One winter's evening, not very long after Christmas, the Colonel made a discovery. It alarmed him a little; for it suggested to his cocksure mind that he did not understand *all* his children as comprehensively as he imagined.

Between five o'clock tea and dinner—that magic hour when lessons were over and the big house was full of shadows and mystery—there came a timid knock at the study door.

"Come in," growled the soldier in his deepest voice, and a little girl's face, wreathed in tumbling brown hair, poked itself hesitatingly through the opening.

The Colonel did not like being disturbed at this hour, and everybody in the house knew it; but the spell of Christmas holidays was still somehow in the air, and the customary order was not yet fully re-established. Moreover, when he saw who the intruder was, his growl modified itself into a sort of common sternness that yet was not cleverly enough simulated to deceive the really intuitive little person who now stood inside the room.

"Well, Nixie, child, what do you want now?"

"Please, father, will you—we wondered if—"

A chorus of whispers issued from the other side of the door:

"Go on, silly!"

"Out with it!"

"You promised you would, Nixie."

". . . if you would come and play Rabbits with us?" came the words in a desperate rush, with laughter not far behind.

The big man with the fierce white moustaches glared over the top of his glasses at the intruders as if amazed beyond belief at the audacity of the request.

"Rabbits!" he exclaimed, as though the mere word ought to have caused an instant explosion. "Rabbits!"

"Oh, *please* do."

"Rabbits at this time of night!" he repeated. "I never heard of such a thing. Why, all good rabbits are asleep in their holes by now. And you ought to be in yours too by rights, I'm sure."

"We don't sleep in holes, father," said the owner of the brown hair, who was acting as leader.

"And there's still a nour before bedtime, *really*," added a voice in the rear.

The big man slowly put his glasses down and looked at his watch. He looked very savage, but of course it was all pretence, and the children knew it. "If he was *really* cross he'd pretend to be nice," they whispered to each other, with merciless perception.

"Well—" he began. But he who hesitates, with children, is lost. The door flung open wide, and the troop poured into the room in a medley of long black legs, flying hair and outstretched hands. They surrounded the table, swarmed upon his big knees, shut his stupid old book, tried on his glasses, kissed him, and fell to discussing the game breathlessly all at once, as though it had already begun.

This, of course, ended the battle, and the big man had to play the part of the Monster Rabbit in a wonderful game of his own invention. But when, at length, it was all over, and they were gathered panting round the fire of blazing logs in the hall, the Monster Rabbit—the only one with any breath at his command—looked up and spoke.

"Where's Jimbo?" he asked.

"Upstairs."

"Why didn't he come and play too?"

"He didn't want to."

"Why? What's he doing?"

Several answers were forthcoming.

"Nothing in p'tickler."

"Talking to the furniture when I last saw him."

"Just thinking, as usual, or staring in the fire."

None of the answers seemed to satisfy the Monster Rabbit, for when he kissed them a little later and said good-night, he gave orders, with a graver face, for Jimbo to be sent down to the study before he went to bed. Moreover, he called him "James," which was a sure sign of parental displeasure.

"James, why didn't you come and play with your brothers and sisters just now?" asked the Colonel, as a dreamy-eyed boy of about eight, with a mop of dark hair and a wistful expression, came slowly forward into the room.

"I was in the middle of making pictures."

"Where—what—making pictures?"

"In the fire."

"James," said the Colonel in a serious tone, "don't you know that you are getting too old now for that sort of thing? If you dream so much, you'll fall asleep altogether some fine day, and never wake up again. Just think what that means!"

The child smiled faintly and moved up confidingly between his father's knees, staring into his eyes without the least sign of fear. But he said nothing in reply. His thoughts were far away, and it seemed as if the effort to bring them back into the study and to a consideration of his father's words was almost beyond his power.

"You must run about more," pursued the soldier, rubbing his big hands together briskly, "and join your brothers and sisters in their games. Lie about in the summer and dream a bit if you like, but now it's winter, you must be more active, and make your blood circulate healthily,—er—and all that sort of thing."

The words were kindly spoken, but the voice and manner rather deliberate. Jimbo began to look a little troubled, as his father watched him.

"Come now, little man," he said more gently, "what's the matter, eh?" He drew the boy close to him. "Tell me all about it, and what it is you're always thinking about so much."

Jimbo brought back his mind with a tremendous effort, and said, "I don't like the winter. It's so dark and full of horrid things. It's all ice and shadows, so—so I go away and think of what I like, and other places—"

"Nonsense!" interrupted his father briskly; "winter's a capital time for boys. What in the world d'ye mean, I wonder?"

He lifted the child on to his knee and stroked his hair, as though he were patting the flank of a horse. Jimbo took no notice of the interruption or of the caress, but went on saying what he had to say, though with eyes a little more clouded.

"Winter's like going into a long black tunnel, you see. It's downhill to Christmas, of course, and then uphill all the way to the summer holidays. But the uphill part's so slow that—"

"Tut, tut!" laughed the Colonel in spite of himself; "you mustn't have such thoughts. Those are a baby's notions. They're silly, silly, silly."

"Do you *really* think so, father?" continued the boy, as if politeness demanded some recognition of his father's remarks, but otherwise anxious only to say what was in his mind. "You wouldn't think them silly if you really knew. But, of course, there's no one to tell you in the stable, so you *can't* know. You've never seen the funny big people rushing past you and laughing through their long hair when the wind blows so loud. *I* know several of them almost to speak to, but you hear only wind. And the other things with tiny legs that skate up and down the slippery moonbeams, without ever tumbling off—they aren't silly a

ALGERNON BLACKWOOD

bit, only they don't like dogs and noise. And I've seen the furniture"—he pronounced it furchinur—"dancing about in the day-nursery when it thought it was alone, and I've heard it talking at night. I know the big cupboard's voice quite well. It's just like a drum, only rougher. . ."

The Colonel shook his head and frowned severely, staring hard at his son. But though their eyes met, the boy hardly saw him. Far away at the other end of the dark Tunnel of the Months he saw the white summer sunshine lying over gardens full of nodding flowers. Butterflies were flitting across meadows yellow with buttercups, and he saw the fascinating rings upon the lawn where the Fairy People held their dances in the moonlight; he heard the wind call to him as it ran on along by the hedgerows, and saw the gentle pressure of its swift feet upon the standing hay; streams were murmuring under shady trees; birds were singing; and there were echoes of sweeter music still that he could not understand, but loved all the more perhaps on that account. . .

"Yes," announced the Colonel later that evening to his wife, spreading his hands out as he spoke. "Yes, my dear, I *have* made a discovery, and an alarming one. You know, I'm rarely at fault where the children are concerned—and I've noted all the symptoms with unusual care. James, my dear, is an imaginative boy."

He paused to note the effect of his words, but seeing none, continued:

"I regret to be obliged to say it, but it's a fact beyond dispute. His head is simply full of things, and he talked to me this evening about tunnels and slippery moonlight till I very nearly lost my temper altogether. Now, the boy will never make a man unless we take him in hand properly at once. We must get him a governess, or something, without delay. Just fancy, if he grew up into a poet or one of these—these—"

In his distress the soldier could only think of horse-terms, which did not seem quite the right language. He stuck altogether, and kept repeating the favourite gesture with his open hand, staring at his wife over his glasses as he did so.

But the mother never argued.

"He's very young still," she observed quietly, "and, as you have always said, he's not a bit like other boys, remember."

"Exactly what I say. Now that your eyes are opened to the actual state of affairs, I'm satisfied."

"We'll get a sensible nursery-governess at once," added the mother.

"A practical one?"

"Yes, dear."

"Hard-headed?"

"Yes."

"And well educated?"

"Yes."

"And—er—firm with children. She'll do for the lot, then."

"If possible."

"And a young woman who doesn't go in for poetry, and dreaming, and all that kind of flummery."

"Of course, dear."

"Capital. I felt sure you would agree with me," he went on. "It'd be no end of a pity if Jimbo grew up an ass. At present he hardly knows the difference between a roadster and a racer. He's going into the army, too," he added by way of climax, "and you know, my dear, the army would never stand *that*!"

"Never," said the mother quietly, and the conversation came to an end.

Meanwhile, the subject of these remarks was lying wide awake upstairs in the bed with the yellow iron railing round it. His elder brother was asleep in the opposite corner of the room, snoring peacefully. He could just see the brass knobs of the bedstead as the dying firelight quivered and shone on them. The walls and ceiling were draped in shadows that altered their shapes from time to time as the coals dropped softly into the grate. Gradually the fire sank, and the room darkened. A feeling of delight and awe stole into his heart.

Jimbo loved these early hours of the night before sleep came. He felt no fear of the dark; its mystery thrilled his soul; but he liked the summer dark, with its soft, warm silences better than the chill winter shadows. Presently the firelight sprang up into a brief flame and then died away altogether with an odd little gulp. He knew the sound well; he often watched the fire out, and now, as he lay in bed waiting for he knew not what, the moonlight filtered in through the baize curtains and gradually gave to the room a wholly new character.

Jimbo sat up in bed and listened. The house was very still. He slipped into his red dressing-gown and crept noiselessly over to the window. For a moment he paused by his brother's bed to make sure that he really was asleep; then, evidently satisfied, he drew aside a corner of the curtain and peered out.

"Oh!" he said, drawing in his breath with delight, and again "oh!"

It was difficult to understand why the sea of white moonlight that covered the lawn should fill him with such joy, and at the same time

ALGERNON BLACKWOOD

bring a lump into his throat. It made him feel as if he were swelling out into something very much greater than the actual limits of his little person. And the sensation was one of mingled pain and delight, too intense for him to feel for very long. The unhappiness passed gradually away, he always noticed, and the happiness merged after a while into a sort of dreamy ecstasy in which he neither thought nor wished much, but was conscious only of one single unmanageable yearning.

The huge cedars on the lawn reared themselves up like giants in silver cloaks, and the horse-chestnut—the Umbrella Tree, as the children called it—loomed with motionless branches that were frosted and shining. Beyond it, in a blue mist of moonlight and distance, lay the kitchen-garden; he could just make out the line of the high wall where the fruit-trees grew. Immediately below him the gravel of the carriage drive sparkled with frost.

The bars of the windows were cold to his hands, yet he stood there for a long time with his nose flattened against the pane and his bare feet on the cane chair. He felt both happy and sad; his heart longed dreadfully for something he had not got, something that seemed out of his reach because he could not name it. No one seemed to believe all the things he *knew* in quite the same way as he did. His brothers and sisters played up to a certain point, and then put the things aside as if they had only been assumed for the time and were not real. To him they were always real. His father's words, too, that evening had sorely puzzled him when he came to think over them afterwards: "They're a baby's notions. . . They're silly, silly, silly." Were these things real or were they not? And, as he pondered, yearning dumbly, as only these little souls can yearn, the wistfulness in his heart went out to meet the moonlight in the air. Together they wove a spell that seemed to summon before him a fairy of the night, who whispered an answer into his heart: "We are real so long as you believe in us. It is your imagination that makes us real and gives us life. Please, never, never stop believing."

Jimbo was not quite sure that he understood the message, but he liked it all the same, and felt comforted. So long as they believed in one another, the rest did not matter very much after all. And when at last, shivering with cold, he crept back to bed, it was only to find through the Gates of Sleep a more direct way to the things he had been thinking about, and to wander for the rest of the night, unwatched and free, through the wonders of an Enchanted Land.

Jimbo, as his father had said, was an imaginative child. Most children are—more or less; and he was "more," at least, "more" than his brothers and sisters. The Colonel thought he had made a penetrating discovery, but his wife had known it always. His head, indeed, was "full of things,"—things that, unless trained into a channel where they could be controlled and properly schooled, would certainly interfere with his success in a practical world, and be a source of mingled pain and joy to him all through life. To have trained these forces, ever bursting out towards creation, in his little soul,—to have explained, interpreted, and dealt fairly by them, would perhaps have been the best and wisest way; to have suppressed them altogether, cleaned them out by the process of substitution, this might have succeeded too in less measure; but to turn them into a veritable rout of horror by the common method of "frightening the nonsense out of the boy," this was surely the very worst way of dealing with such a case, and the most cruel. Yet, this was the method adopted by the Colonel in the robust good-nature of his heart, and the utter ignorance of his soul.

So it came about that three months later, when May was melting into June, Miss Ethel Lake arrived upon the scene as a result of the Colonel's blundering good intentions. She brought with her a kind disposition, a supreme ignorance of unordinary children, a large store of self-confidence—and a corded yellow tin box.

II

Miss Lake Comes—and Goes

The conversation took place suddenly one afternoon, and no one knew anything about it except the two who took part in it: the Colonel asked the governess to try and knock the nonsense out of Jimbo's head, and the governess promised eagerly to do her very best. It was her first "place"; and by "nonsense" they both understood imagination. True enough, Jimbo's mother had given her rather different instructions as to the treatment of the boy, but she mistook the soldier's bluster for authority, and deemed it best to obey him. This was her first mistake.

In reality she was not devoid of imaginative insight; it was simply that her anxiety to prove a success permitted her better judgment to be overborne by the Colonel's boisterous manner.

The wisdom of the mother was greater than that of her husband. For the safe development of that tender and imaginative little boy of hers, she had been at great pains to engage a girl—a clergyman's daughter— who possessed sufficient sympathy with the poetic and dreamy nature to be of real help to him; for true help, she knew, can only come from true understanding. And Miss Lake was a good girl. She was entirely well-meaning—which is the beginning of well-doing, and her principal weakness lay in her judgment, which led her to obey the Colonel too literally.

"She seems most sensible," he declared to his wife.

"Yes, dear."

"And practical."

"I think so."

"And firm and—er—wise with children."

"I hope so."

"Just the sort for young Jimbo," added the Colonel with decision.

"I trust so; she's a little young, perhaps."

"Possibly, but one can't get everything," said her husband, in his horse-and-dog voice. "A year with her should clean out that fanciful brain of his, and prepare him for school with other boys. He'll be all right once he gets to school. My dear," he added, spreading out his right hand, fingers extended, "you've made a most wise selection. I congratulate you. I'm delighted."

"I'm so glad."

"Capital, I repeat, capital. You're a clever little woman. I knew you'd find the right party, once I showed you how the land lay."

The Empty House, that stood in its neglected garden not far from the Park gates, was built on a point of land that entered wedgewise into the Colonel's estate. Though something of an eyesore, therefore, he could do nothing with it.

To the children it had always been an object of peculiar, though not unwholesome, mystery. None of them cared to pass it on a stormy day— the wind made such odd noises in its empty corridors and rooms—and they refused point-blank to go within hailing distance of it after dark. But in Jimbo's imagination it was especially haunted, and if he had ceased to reveal to the others what he *knew* went on under its roof, it was only because they were unable to follow him, and were inclined to greet his extravagant recitals with "Now, Jimbo, you know *perfectly* well you're only making up."

The House had been empty for many years; but, to the children, it had been empty since the beginning of the world, since what they called the "*very* beginning." They believed—well, each child believed according to his own mind and powers, but there was at least one belief they all held in common: for it was generally accepted as an article of faith that the Indians, encamped among the shrubberies on the back lawn, secretly buried their dead behind the crumbling walls of its weedy garden—the "dead" provided by the children's battles, be it understood. Wakeful ears in the night-nursery had heard strange sounds coming from that direction when the windows were open on hot summer nights; and the gardener, supreme authority on all that happened in the night (since they believed that he sat up to watch the vegetables and fruit-trees ripen, and never went to bed at all), was evidently of the same persuasion.

When appealed to for an explanation of the mournful wind-voices, he knew what was expected of him, and rose manfully to the occasion.

"It's either them Redskins aburyin' wot you killed of 'em yesterday," he declared, pointing towards the Empty House with a bit of broken flower-pot, "or else it's the ones you killed last week, and who was always astealin' of my strorbriz." He looked very wise as he said this,

ALGERNON BLACKWOOD

and his wand of office—a dirty trowel—which he held in his hand, gave him tremendous dignity.

"That's just what *we* thought, and of course if you say so too, that settles it," said Nixie.

"It's more'n likely, missie, leastways from wot you describes, which it is a hempty house all the same, though I can't say as I've heard no sounds, not very distinct that is, myself."

The gardener may have been anxious to hedge a bit, for fear of a scolding from headquarters, but his cryptic remarks pleased the children greatly, because it showed, they thought, that they knew more than the gardener did.

Thus the Empty House remained an object of somewhat dreadful delight, lending a touch of wonderland to that part of the lane where it stood, and forming the background for many an enchanting story over the nursery fire in winter-time. It appealed vividly to their imaginations, especially to Jimbo's. Its dark windows, without blinds, were sometimes full of faces that retreated the moment they were looked at. That tangled ivy did not grow over the roof so thickly for nothing; and those high elms on the western side had not been planted years ago in a semicircle without a reason. Thus, at least, the children argued, not knowing exactly what they meant, nor caring much, so long as they proved to their own satisfaction that the place was properly haunted, and therefore worthy of their attention.

It was natural they should lead Miss Lake in that direction on one of their first walks together, and it was natural, too, that she should at once discover from their manner that the place was of some importance to them.

"What a queer-looking old house," she remarked, when they turned the corner of the lane and it came into view. "Almost a ruin, isn't it?"

The children exchanged glances. A "ruin" did not seem the right sort of word at all; and, besides, was a little disrespectful. Also, they were not sure whether the new governess ought to be told everything so soon. She had not really won their confidence yet. After a slight pause—and a children's pause is the most eloquent imaginable—Nixie, being the eldest, said in a stiff little voice: "It's the Empty House, Miss Lake. *We* know it very well indeed."

"It looks empty," observed Miss Lake briskly.

"But it's not a ruin, of course," added the child, with the cold dignity of chosen spokesman.

"Oh!" said the governess, quite missing the point. She was talking lightly on the surface of things, wholly ignorant of the depths beneath her feet, intuition with her having always been sternly repressed.

"It's a gamekeeper's cottage, or something like that, I suppose," she said.

"Oh, no; it isn't a bit."

"Doesn't it belong to your father, then?"

"No. It's somebody else's, you see."

"Then you can't have it pulled down?"

"Rather not! Of course not!" exclaimed several indignant voices at once.

Miss Lake perceived for the first time that it held more than ordinary importance in their mind.

"Tell me about it," she said. "What is its history, and who used to live in it?"

There came another pause. The children looked into each others' faces. They gazed at the blue sky overhead; then they stared at the dusty road at their feet. But no one volunteered an answer. Miss Lake, they felt, was approaching the subject in an offensive manner.

"Why are you all so mysterious about it?" she went on. "It's only a tumble-down old place, and must be very draughty to live in, even for a gamekeeper."

Silence.

"Come, children, don't you hear me? I'm asking you a question."

A couple of startled birds flew out of the ivy with a great whirring of wings. This was followed by a faint sound of rumbling, that seemed to come from the interior of the house. Outside all was still, and the hot sunshine lay over everything. The sound was repeated. The children looked at each other with large, expectant eyes. Something in the house was moving—was coming nearer.

"Have you *all* lost your tongues?" asked the governess impatiently.

"But you see," Nixie said at length, "somebody *does* live in it now."

"And who is he?"

"I didn't say it was a *man*."

"Whoever it is—tell me about the person," persisted Miss Lake.

"There's really nothing to tell," replied the child, without looking up.

"Oh, but there must be something," declared the logical young governess, "or you wouldn't object so much to its being pulled down."

Nixie looked puzzled, but Jimbo came to the rescue at once.

"But *you* wouldn't understand if we did tell you," he said, in a slow, respectful voice. His tone held a touch of that indescribable scorn heard sometimes in a child's tone—the utter contempt for the stupid grown-up creature. Miss Lake noticed, and felt annoyed. She recognised that she was not getting on well with the children, and it piqued her. She remembered the Colonel's words about "knocking the nonsense out" of James' head, and she saw that her first opportunity, in fact her first real test, was at hand.

"And why, pray, should I not understand?" she asked, with some sharpness. "Is the mystery so *very* great?"

For some reason the duty of spokesman now devolved unmistakably upon Jimbo; and very seriously too, he accepted the task, standing with his feet firmly planted in the road and his hands in his trousers' pockets.

"You see, Miss Lake," he began gravely, "we know such a lot of Things in there, that they might not like us to tell you about them. They don't know you yet. If they did it might be different. But—but—you see, it isn't."

This was rather crushing to the aspiring educator, and the Colonel's instructions gained additional point in the light of the boy's explanation.

"Fiddlesticks!" she laughed, "there's probably nothing at all in there, except rats and cobwebs. 'Things,' indeed!"

"I knew you wouldn't understand," said Jimbo coolly, with no sign of being offended. "How could you?" He glanced at his sisters, gaining so much support from their enigmatical faces that he added, for their especial benefit, "How could she?"

"The gard'ner said so too," chimed in a younger sister, with a vague notion that their precious Empty House was being robbed of its glory.

"Yes; but, James, dear, I do understand perfectly," continued Miss Lake more gently, and wisely ignoring the reference to the authority of the kitchen-garden. "Only, you see, I cannot really encourage you in such nonsense—"

"It isn't nonsense," interrupted Jimbo, with heat.

"But, believe me, children, it *is* nonsense. How do you know that there's anything inside? You've never been there!"

"You can know perfectly well what's inside a thing without having gone there," replied Jimbo with scorn. "At least, *we* can."

Miss Lake changed her tack a little—fatally, as it appeared afterwards.

"I know at any rate," she said with decision, "that there's nothing good in there. Whatever there may be is bad, thoroughly bad, and not fit for you to play with."

The other children moved away, but Jimbo stood his ground. They were all angry, disappointed, sore hurt and offended. But Jimbo suddenly began to feel something else besides anger and vexation. It was a new point of view to him that the Empty House might contain bad things as well as good, or perhaps, only bad things. His imagination seized upon the point at once and set to work vigorously to develop it. This was his way with all such things, and he could not prevent it.

"Bad Things?" he repeated, looking up at the governess. "You mean Things that could hurt?"

"Yes, of course," she said, noting the effect of her words and thinking how pleased the Colonel would be later, when he heard it. "Things that might run out and catch you some day when you're passing here alone, and take you back a prisoner. Then you'd be a prisoner in the Empty House all your life. Think of that!"

Miss Lake mistook the boy's silence as proof that she was taking the right line. She enlarged upon this view of the matter, now she was so successfully launched, and described the *Inmate of the House* with such wealth of detail that she felt sure her listener would never have anything to do with the place again, and that she had "knocked out" this particular bit of "nonsense" for ever and a day.

But to Jimbo it was a new and horrible idea that the Empty House, haunted hitherto only by rather jolly and wonderful Red Indians, contained a Monster who might take him prisoner, and the thought made him feel afraid. The mischief had, of course, been done, and the terror in his eyes was unmistakable, when the foolish governess saw her mistake. Retreat was impossible: the boy was shaking with fear; and not all Miss Lake's genuine sympathy, or Nixie's explanations and soothings, were able to relieve his mind of its new burden.

Hitherto Jimbo's imagination had loved to dwell upon the pleasant side of things invisible; but now he had been severely frightened, and his imagination took a new turn. Not only the Empty House, but all his inner world, to which it was in some sense the key, underwent a distressing change. His sense of horror had been vividly aroused.

The governess would willingly have corrected her mistake, but was, of course, powerless to do so. Bitterly she regretted her tactlessness and folly. But she could do nothing, and to add to her distress, she saw that

ALGERNON BLACKWOOD

Jimbo shrank from her in a way that could not long escape the watchful eye of the mother. But, if the boy shed tears of fear that night in his bed, it must in justice be told that she, for her part, cried bitterly in her own room, not that she had endangered her "place," but that she had done a cruel injury to a child, and that she was helpless to undo it. For she loved children, though she was quite unsuited to take care of them. Her just reward, however, came swiftly upon her.

A few nights later, when Jimbo and Nixie were allowed to come down to dessert, the wind was heard to make a queer moaning sound in the ivy branches that hung over the dining-room windows. Jimbo heard it too. He held his breath for a minute; then he looked round the table in a frightened way, and the next minute gave a scream and burst into tears. He ran round and buried his face in his father's arms.

After the tears came the truth. It was a bad thing for Miss Ethel Lake, this little sighing of the wind and the ivy leaves, for the Djin of terror she had thoughtlessly evoked swept into the room and introduced himself to the parents without her leave.

"What new nonsense is this now?" growled the soldier, leaving his walnuts and lifting the boy on to his knee. "He shouldn't come down till he's a little older, and knows how to behave."

"What's the matter, darling child?" asked the mother, drying his eyes tenderly.

"I heard the bad Things crying in the Empty House."

"The Empty House is a mile away from here!" snorted the Colonel.

"Then it's come nearer," declared the frightened boy.

"Who told you there were bad things in the Empty House?" asked the mother.

"Yes, who told you, indeed, I should like to know!" demanded the Colonel.

And then it all came out. The Colonel's wife was very quiet, but very determined. Miss Lake went back to the clerical family whence she had come, and the children knew her no more.

"I'm glad," said Nixie, expressing the verdict of the nursery. "I thought she was awfully stupid."

"She wasn't a real lake at all," declared another, "she was only a sort of puddle."

Jimbo, however, said little, and the Colonel likewise held his peace.

But the governess, whether she was a lake or only a puddle, left her mark behind her. The Empty House was no longer harmless. It had a new lease of life. It was tenanted by some one who could never have friendly relations with children. The weeds in the old garden took on fantastic shapes; figures hid behind the doors and crept about the passages; the rooks in the high elms became birds of ill-omen; the ivy bristled upon the walls, and the trivial explanations of the gardener were no longer satisfactory.

Even in bright sunshine a Shadow lay crouching upon the broken roof. At any moment it might leap into life, and with immense striding legs chase the children down to the very Park gates.

There was no need to enforce the decree that the Empty House was a forbidden land. The children of their own accord declared it out of bounds, and avoided it as carefully as if all the wild animals from the Zoo were roaming its gardens, hungry and unchained.

III

The Shock

One immediate result of Miss Lake's indiscretion was that the children preferred to play on the other side of the garden, the side farthest from the Empty House. A spiked railing here divided them from a field in which cows disported themselves, and as bulls also sometimes were admitted to the cows, the field was strictly out of bounds.

In this spiked railing, not far from the great shrubberies where the Indians increased and multiplied, there was a swinging gate. The children swung on it whenever they could. They called it Express Trains, and the fact that it was forbidden only added to their pleasure. When opened at its widest it would swing them with a rush through the air, past the pillars with a click, out into the field, and then back again into the garden. It was bad for the hinges, and it was also bad for the garden, because it was frequently left open after these carnivals, and the cows got in and trod the flowers down. The children were not afraid of the cows, but they held the bull in great horror. And these trivial things have been mentioned here because of the part they played in Jimbo's subsequent adventures.

It was only ten days or so after Miss Lake's sudden departure when Jimbo managed one evening to elude the vigilance of his lawful guardians, and wandered off unnoticed among the laburnums on the front lawn. From the laburnums he passed successfully to the first laurel shrubbery, and thence he executed a clever flank movement and entered the carriage drive in the rear. The rest was easy, and he soon found himself at the Lodge gate.

For some moments he peered through the iron grating, and pondered on the seductiveness of the dusty road and of the ditch beyond. To his surprise he found, presently, that the gate was moving outwards; it was yielding to his weight. One thing leads easily to another sometimes, and the open gate led easily on to the seductive road. The result was that a minute later Jimbo was chasing butterflies along the green lane, and throwing stones into the water of the ditch.

It was the evening of a hot summer's day, and the butterflies were still out in force. Jimbo's delight was intense. The joy of finding himself alone where he had no right to be put everything else out of his head, and for some time he wandered on, oblivious of all but the intoxicating sense of freedom and the difficulty of choosing between so many butterflies and such a magnificently dirty ditch.

At first he yielded to the seductions of the ditch. He caught a big, sleepy beetle and put it on a violet leaf, and sent it sailing out to sea; and when it landed on the farther shore he found a still bigger leaf, and sent it forth on a voyage in another direction, with a cargo of daisy petals, and a hairy caterpillar for a bo'sun's mate. But, just as the vessel was getting under way, a butterfly of amazing brilliance floated past insolently under his very nose. Leaving the beetle and the caterpillar to navigate the currents as best they could, he at once gave chase. Cap in hand, he flew after the butterfly down the lane, and a dozen times when his cap was just upon it, it sailed away sideways without the least effort and escaped him.

Then, suddenly, the lane took a familiar turning; the ditch stopped abruptly; the hedge on his right fell away altogether; the butterfly danced out of sight into a field, and Jimbo found himself face to face with the one thing in the whole world that could, at that time, fill him with abject terror—the Empty House.

He came to a full stop in the middle of the road and stared up at the windows. He realised for the first time that he was alone, and that it was possible for brilliant sunshine, even on a cloudless day, to become somehow lustreless and dull. The walls showed a deep red in the sunset light. The house was still as the grave. His feet were rooted to the ground, and it seemed as if he could not move a single muscle; and as he stood there, the blood ebbing quickly from his heart, the words of the governess a few days before rushed back into his mind, and turned his fear into a dreadful, all-possessing horror. In another minute the battered door would slowly open and the horrible Inmate come out to seize him. Already there was a sound of something moving within, and as he gazed, fascinated with terror, a shuddering movement ran over the ivy leaves hanging down from the roof. Then they parted in the middle, and something—he could not in his agony see what—flew out with a whirring sound into his face, and then vanished over his shoulder towards the fields.

Jimbo did not pause a single second to find out what it was, or to reflect that any ordinary thrush would have made just the same sound. The shock it gave to his heart immediately loosened the muscles of his

ALGERNON BLACKWOOD

little legs, and he ran for his very life. But before he actually began to run he gave one piercing scream for help, and the person he screamed to was the very person who was unwittingly the cause of his distress. It was as though he knew instinctively that the person who had created for him the terror of the Empty House, with its horrible Inmate, was also the person who could properly banish it, and undo the mischief before it was too late. He shrieked for help to the governess, Miss Ethel Lake.

Of course, there was no answer but the noise of the air whistling in his ears as his feet flew over the road in a cloud of dust; there was no friendly butcher's cart, no baker's boy, or farmer with his dog and gun; the road was deserted. There was not even the beetle or the caterpillar; he was beyond reach of help.

Jimbo ran for his life, but unfortunately he ran in the wrong direction. Instead of going the way he had come, where the Lodge gates were ready to receive him not a quarter of a mile away, he fled in the opposite direction.

It so happened that the lane flanked the field where the cows lived; but cows were nothing compared to a Creature from the Empty House, and even bulls seemed friendly. The boy was over the five-barred gate in a twinkling and half-way across the field before he heard a heavy, thunderous sound behind him. Either the Thing had followed him into the field, or it was the bull. As he raced, he managed to throw a glance over his shoulder and saw a huge, dark mass bearing down upon him at terrific speed. It must be the bull, he reflected—the bull grown to the size of an elephant. And it appeared to him to have two immense black wings that flapped at its sides and helped it forward, making a whirring noise like the arms of a great windmill.

This sight added to his speed, but he could not last very much longer. Already his body ached all over, and the frantic effort to get breath nearly choked him.

There, before him, not so very far away now, was the swinging gate. If only he could get there in time to scramble over into the garden, he would be safe. It seemed almost impossible, and behind him, meanwhile, the sound of the following creature came closer and closer; the ground seemed to tremble; he could almost feel the breath on his neck.

The swinging gate was only twenty yards off; now ten; now only five. Now he had reached it—at last. He stretched out his hands to seize the top bar, and in another moment he would have been safe in the garden and within easy reach of the house. But, before he actually touched the iron rail, a sharp, stinging pain shot across his back;—he drew one final breath as he felt himself being lifted, lifted up into the air. The horns had caught him just behind the shoulders!

There seemed to be no pain after the first shock. He rose high into the air, while the bushes and spiked railing he knew so well sank out of sight beneath him, dwindling curiously in size. At first he thought his head must bump against the sky, but suddenly he stopped rising, and the green earth rushed up as if it would strike him in the face. This meant he was sinking again. The gate and railing flew by underneath him, and the next second he fell with a crash upon the soft grass of the lawn—upon the other side. He had been tossed over the gate into the garden, and the bull could no longer reach him.

Before he became wholly unconscious, a composite picture, vivid in its detail, engraved itself deeply, with exceeding swiftness, line by line, upon the waxen tablets of his mind. In this picture the thrush that had flown out of the ivy, the Empty House itself, and its horrible, pursuing Inmate were all somehow curiously mingled together with the black wings of the bull, and with his own sensation of rushing— flying headlong—through space, as he rose and fell in a curve from the creature's horns.

And behind it he was conscious that the real author of it all was somewhere in the shadowy background, looking on as though to watch the result of her unfortunate mistake. Miss Lake, surely, was not very far away. He associated her with the horror of the Empty House as inevitably as taste and smell join together in the memory of a certain food; and the very last thought in his mind, as he sank away into the blackness of unconsciousness, was a sort of bitter surprise that the governess had not turned up to save him before it was actually too late.

Moreover, a certain sense of disappointment mingled with the terror of the shock; for he was dimly aware that Miss Lake had not acted as worthily as she might have done, and had not played the game as well as might have been expected of her. And, somehow, it didn't all seem quite fair.

IV

On the Edge of Unconsciousness

Jimbo had fallen on his head. Inside that head lay the mass of highly sensitive matter called the brain, on which were recorded, of course, the impressions of everything that had yet come to him in life. A severe shock, such as he had just sustained, was bound to throw these impressions into confusion and disorder, jumbling them up into new and strange combinations, obliterating some, and exaggerating others. Jimbo himself was helpless in the matter; he could exercise no control over their antics until the doctors had once again reduced them to order; he would have to wander, lost and lonely, through the comparative chaos of disproportioned visions, generally known as the region of delirium, until the doctor, assisted by mother nature, restored him once more to normal consciousness.

For a time everything was a blank, but presently he stirred uneasily in the grass, and the pictures graven on the tablets of his mind began to come back to him line by line.

Yet, with certain changes: the bull, for instance, had so far vanished into the background of his thoughts that it had practically disappeared altogether, and he recalled nothing of it but the wings—the huge, flapping wings. Of the creature to whom the wings belonged he had no recollection beyond that it was very large, and that it was chasing him from the Empty House. The pain in his shoulders had also gone; but what remained with undiminished vividness were the sensations of flight without escape, the breathless race up into the sky, and the swift, tumbling drop again through the air on to the lawn.

This impression of rushing through space—short though the actual distance had been—was the dominating memory. All else was apparently oblivion. He forgot where he came from, and he forgot what he had been doing. The events leading up to the catastrophe, indeed everything connected with his existence previously as "Master James," had entirely vanished; and the slate of memory had been wiped so clean that he had forgotten even his own name!

Jimbo was lying, so to speak, on the edge of unconsciousness, and for a time it seemed uncertain whether he would cross the line into the region of delirium and dreams, or fall back again into his natural world. Terror, assisted by the horns of the black bull, had tossed him into the borderland.

His last scream, however, had reached the ears of the ubiquitous gardener, and help was near at hand. He heard voices that seemed to come from beyond the stars, and was aware that shadowy forms were standing over him and talking in whispers. But it was all very unreal; one minute the voices sounded up in the sky, and the next in his very ears, while the figures moved about, sometimes bending over him, sometimes retreating and melting away like shadows on a shifting screen.

Suddenly a blaze of light flashed upon him, and his eyes flew open; he tumbled back for a moment into his normal world. He wasn't on the grass at all, but was lying upon his own bed in the night nursery. His mother was bending over him with a very white face, and a tall man dressed in black stood beside her, holding some kind of shining instrument in his fingers. A little behind them he saw Nixie, shading a lamp with her hand. Then the white face came close over the pillow, and a voice full of tenderness whispered, "My darling boy, don't you know me? It's mother! No one will hurt you. Speak to me, if you can, dear."

She stretched out her hands, and Jimbo knew her and made an effort to answer. But it seemed to him as if his whole body had suddenly become a solid mass of iron, and he could control no part of it; his lips and his hands both refused to move. Before he could make a sign that he had understood and was trying to reply, a fierce flame rushed between them and blinded him, his eyes closed, and he dropped back again into utter darkness. The walls flew asunder and the ceiling melted into air, while the bed sank away beneath him, down, down, down into an abyss of shadows. The lamp in Nixie's hands dwindled into a star, and his mother's anxious face became a tiny patch of white in the distance, blurred out of all semblance of a human countenance. For a time the man in black seemed to hover over the bed as it sank, as though he were trying to follow it down; but it, too, presently joined the general enveloping blackness and lost its outline. The pain had blotted out everything, and the return to consciousness had been only momentary.

Not all the doctors in the world could have made things otherwise. Jimbo was off on his travels at last—travels in which the chief incidents were directly traceable to the causes and details of his accident: the terror of the Empty House, the pursuit of its Inmate, the pain of the bull's horns, and, above all, the flight through the air.

For everything in his subsequent adventures found its inspiration in the events described, and a singular parallel ran ever between the Jimbo upon the bed in the night-nursery and the other emancipated Jimbo wandering in the regions of unconsciousness and delirium.

V

Into the Empty House

The darkness lasted a long time without a break, and when it lifted all recollection of the bedroom scene had vanished.

Jimbo found himself back again on the grass. The swinging gate was just in front of him, but he did not recognise it; no suggestion of "Express Trains" came back to him as his eyes rested without remembrance upon the bars where he had so often swung, in defiance of orders, with his brothers and sisters. Recollection of his home, family, and previous life he had absolutely none; or at least, it was buried so deeply in his inner consciousness that it amounted to the same thing, and he looked out upon the garden, the gate, and the field beyond as upon an entirely new piece of the world.

The stars, he saw, were nearly all gone, and a very faint light was beginning to spread from the woods beyond the field. The eastern horizon was slowly brightening, and soon the night would be gone. Jimbo was glad of this. He began to be conscious of little thrills of expectation, for with the light surely help would also come. The light always brought relief, and he already felt that strange excitement that comes with the first signs of dawn. In the distance cocks were crowing, horses began to stamp in the barns not far away, and a hundred little stirrings of life ran over the surface of the earth as the light crept slowly up the sky and dropped down again upon the world with its message of coming day.

Of course, help would come by the time the sun was really up, and it was partly this certainty, and partly because he was a little too dazed to realise the seriousness of the situation, that prevented his giving way to a fit of fear and weeping. Yet a feeling of vague terror lay only a little way below the surface, and when, a few moments later, he saw that he was no longer alone, and that an odd-looking figure was creeping towards him from the shrubberies, he sprang to his feet, prepared to run unless it at once showed the most friendly intentions.

This figure seemed to have come from nowhere. Apparently it had risen out of the earth. It was too large to have been concealed by the low shrubberies; yet he had not been aware of its approach, and it had appeared without making any noise. Probably it was friendly, he felt, in spite of its curious shape and the stealthy way it had come. At least, he hoped so; and if he could only have told whether it was a man or an animal he would easily have made up his mind. But the uncertain light, and the way it crouched half-hidden behind the bushes, prevented this. So he stood, poised ready to run, and yet waiting, hoping, indeed expecting every minute a sign of friendliness and help.

In this way the two faced each other silently for some time, until the feeling of terror gradually stole deeper into the boy's heart and began to rob him of full power over his muscles. He wondered if he would be able to run when the time came, and whether he could run fast enough. This was how it first showed itself, this suggestion of insidious fear. Would he be able to keep up the start he had? Would it chase him? Would it run like a man or like an animal, on four legs or on two? He wished he could see more clearly what it was. He still stood his ground pluckily, facing it and waiting, but the fear, once admitted to his mind, was gaining strength, and he began to feel cold and shivery. Then suddenly the tension came to an end. In two strides the figure came up close to his side, and the same second Jimbo was lifted off his feet and borne swiftly away across the field.

He felt quite unable to offer the least resistance, and at the same time he felt a sense of relief that something had happened at last. He was still not sure that the figure was unkind; only its shape filled him with a feeling that was certainly the beginning of real horror. It was the shape of a man, he thought, but of a very large and ill-constructed man; for it certainly had moved on two legs and had caught him up in a pair of tremendously strong arms. But there was something else it had besides arms, for a kind of soft cloak hung all round it and wrapped the boy from head to foot, preventing him seeing his captor properly, and at the same time filling his body with a kind of warm drowsiness that mitigated his active fear and made him rather like the sensation of being carried along so easily and so fast.

But was he being carried? The pace they were going was amazing, and he moved as easily as a sailing boat, and with the same swinging motion. Could it be some animal like a horse after all? Jimbo tried to see more, but found it impossible to free himself from the folds of the enveloping substance, and meanwhile they were swinging forward at what seemed a tremendous pace over fields and ditches, through hedges, and down long lanes.

The odours of earth, and dew-drenched grass, and opening flowers came to him. He heard the birds singing, and felt the cool morning air sting his cheeks as they raced along. There was no jolting or jarring, and the figure seemed to cover the ground as lightly as though it hardly touched the earth. It was certainly not a dream, he was sure of that; but the longer they went on the drowsier he became, and the less he wondered whether the figure was going to help him or to do something dreadful to him. He was now thoroughly afraid, and yet, strange contradiction, he didn't care a bit. Let the figure do what it liked; it was only a sort of nightmare person after all, and might vanish as suddenly as it had arrived.

For a long time they raced forward at this great speed, and then with a bump and a crash they stopped suddenly short, and Jimbo felt himself let down upon the solid earth. He tried to free himself at once from the folds of the clinging substance that enveloped him, but, before he could do so and see what his captor was really like, he heard a door slam and felt himself pushed along what seemed to be the hallways of a house. His eyes were clear now and he could see, but the darkness had come down again so thickly that all he could discover was that the figure was urging him along the floor of a large empty hall, and that they were in a dark and empty building.

Jimbo tried hard to see his captor, but the figure, dim enough in the uncertain light, always managed to hide its face and keep itself bunched up in such a way that he could never see more than a great, dark mass of a body, from which long legs and arms shot out like telescopes, draped in a sort of clinging cloak. Now that the rapid motion through the air had ceased, the boy's drowsiness passed a little, and he began to shiver with fear and to feel that the tears could not be kept back much longer.

Probably in another minute he would have started to run for his life, when a new sound caught his ears and made him listen intently, while a feeling of wonder and delight caught his heart, and made him momentarily forget the figure pushing him forward from behind.

Was it the wind he heard? Or was it the voices of children all singing together very low? It was a gentle, sighing sound that rose and fell with mournful modulations and seemed to come from the very centre of the building; it held, too, a strange, far-away murmur, like the surge of a faint breeze moving in the tree-tops. It might be the wind playing round the walls of the building, or it might be children singing in hushed voices. One minute he thought it was outside the house, and

ALGERNON BLACKWOOD

the next he was certain it came from somewhere in the upper part of the building. He glanced up, and fancied for one moment that he saw in the darkness a crowd of little faces peering down at him over the banisters, and that as they disappeared he heard the sound of many little feet moving, and then a door hurriedly closing. But a push from the figure behind that nearly sent him sprawling at the foot of the stairs, prevented his hearing very clearly, and the light was far too dim to let him feel sure of what he had seen.

They passed quickly along deserted corridors and through winding passages. No one seemed about. The interior of the house was chilly, and the keen air nipped. After going up several flights of stairs they stopped at last in front of a door, and before Jimbo had a moment to turn and dash downstairs again past the figure, as he had meant to do, he was pushed violently forward into a room.

The door slammed after him, and he heard the heavy tread of the figure as it went down the staircase again into the bottom of the house. Then he saw that the room was full of light and of small moving beings.

Curiosity and astonishment now for a moment took the place of fear, and Jimbo, with a thumping heart and clenched fists, stood and stared at the scene before him. He stiffened his little legs and leaned against the wall for support, but he felt full of fight in case anything happened, and with wide-open eyes he tried to take in the whole scene at once and be ready for whatever might come.

But there seemed no immediate cause for alarm, and when he realised that the beings in the room were apparently children, and only children, his rather mixed sensations of astonishment and fear gave place to an emotion of overpowering shyness. He became exceedingly embarrassed, for he was surrounded by children of all ages and sizes, staring at him just as hard as he was staring at them.

The children, he began to take in, were all dressed in black; they looked frightened and unhappy; their bodies were thin and their faces very white. There was something else about them he could not quite name, but it inspired him with the same sense of horror that he had felt in the arms of the Figure who had trapped him. For he now realised definitely that he had been trapped; and he also began to realise for the first time that, though he still had the body of a little boy, his way of thinking and judging was sometimes more like that of a grown-up person. The two alternated, and the result was an odd confusion; for sometimes he felt like a child and thought like a man, while at others he felt like a man and thought like a child. Something had gone wrong, very much wrong; and, as he watched this group of silent children facing him, he knew suddenly that what was just beginning to happen to him *had happened to them long, long ago*.

For they looked as if they had been a long, long time in the world, yet their bodies had not kept pace with their minds. Something had happened to stop the growth of the body, while allowing the mind to go on developing. The bodies were not stunted or deformed; they were well-formed, nice little children's bodies, but the minds within them were grown-up, and the incongruity was distressing. All this he suddenly realised in a flash, intuitively, just as though it had been most elaborately explained to him; yet he could not have put the least part of it into words or have explained what he saw and felt to another.

He saw that they had the hands and figures of children, the heads of children, the unlined faces and smooth foreheads of children, but their gestures, and something in their movements, belonged to grown-up people, and the expression of their eyes in meaning and intelligence was the expression of old people and not of children. And the expression in the eyes of every one of them he saw was the expression of terror and of pain. The effect was so singular that he seemed face to face with an entirely new order of creatures: a child's features with a man's eyes; a child's figure with a woman's movements; full-grown souls cramped and cribbed in absurdly inadequate bodies and little, puny frames; the old trying uncouthly to express itself in the young.

The grown-up, old portion of him had been uppermost as he stared and received these impressions, but now suddenly it passed away, and he felt as a little boy again. He glanced quickly down at his own little body in the alpaca knickerbockers and sailor blouse, and then, with a sigh of relief, looked up again at the strange group facing him. So far, at any rate, he had not changed, and there was nothing yet to suggest that he was becoming like them in appearance at least.

With his back against the door he faced the roomful of children who stood there motionless and staring; and as he looked, wild feelings rushed over him and made him tremble. Who was he? Where had he come from? Where in the world had he spent the other years of his life, the forgotten years? There seemed to be no one to whom he could go for comfort, no one to answer questions; and there was such a lot he wanted to ask. He seemed to be so much older, and to know so much more than he ought to have known, and yet to have forgotten so much that he ought not to have forgotten.

His loss of memory, however, was of course only partial. He had forgotten his own identity, and all the people with whom he had so far in life had to do; yet at the same time he was dimly conscious that he had just left all these people, and that some day he would find them again. It was only the surface-layers of memory that had vanished, and these had not vanished for ever, but only sunk down a little below the horizon.

Then, presently, the children began to range themselves in rows between him and the opposite wall, without once taking their horrible, intelligent eyes off him as they moved. He watched them with growing dread, but at last his curiosity became so strong that it overcame everything else, and in a voice that he meant to be very brave, but that sounded hardly above a whisper, he said:

"Who are you? And what's been done to you?"

The answer came at once in a whisper as low as his own, though he could not distinguish who spoke:

"Listen and you shall know. You, too, are now one of us."

Immediately the children began a slow, impish sort of dance before him, moving almost with silent feet over the boards, yet with a sedateness and formality that had none of the unconscious grace of children. And, as they danced, they sang, but in voices so low, that it was more like the mournful sighing of wind among branches than human voices. It was the sound he had already heard outside the building.

> *"We are the children of the whispering night,*
> *Who live eternally in dreadful fright*
> *Of stories told us in the grey twilight*
> *By*—nurserymaids!*
>
> *We are the children of a winter's day;*
> *Under our breath we chant this mournful lay;*
> *We dance with phantoms and with shadows play,*
> *And have no rest.*
>
> *We have no joy in any children's game,*
> *For happiness to us is but a name,*
> *Since Terror kissed us with his lips of flame*
> *In wicked jest.*

We hear the little voices in the wind
Singing of freedom we may never find,
Victims of fate so cruelly unkind,
We are unblest.

We hear the little footsteps in the rain
Running to help us, though they run in vain,
Tapping in hundreds on the window-pane
In vain behest.

We are the children of the whispering night,
Who dwell unrescued in eternal fright
Of stories told us in the dim twilight
By—nurserymaids!"

The plaintive song and the dance ceased together, and before Jimbo could find any words to clothe even one of the thoughts that crowded through his mind, he saw them moving towards a door he had not hitherto noticed on the other side of the room. A moment later they had opened it and passed out, sedate, mournful, unhurried; and the boy found that in some way he could not understand the light had gone with them, and he was standing with his back against the wall in almost total darkness.

Once out of the room, no sound followed them, and he crossed over and tried the handle of the door. It was locked. Then he went back and tried the other door; that, too, was locked. He was shut in. There was no longer any doubt as to the Figure's intentions; he was a prisoner, trapped like an animal in a cage.

The only thought in his mind just then was an intense desire for freedom. Whatever happened he must escape. He crossed the floor to the only window in the room; it was without blinds, and he looked out. But instantly he recoiled with a fresh and overpowering sense of helplessness, for it was three storeys from the ground, and down below in the shadows he saw a paved courtyard that rendered jumping utterly out of the question.

He stood for a long time, fighting down the tears, and staring as if his heart would break at the field and trees beyond. A high wall enclosed the yard, but beyond that was freedom and open space. Feelings of loneliness and helplessness, terror and dismay overwhelmed him. His eyes burned and smarted, yet, strange to say, the tears now refused to come and bring him relief. He could only stand there with his elbows on the window-sill, and watch the outline of the trees and hedges grow clearer and clearer as the light drew across the sky, and the moment of sunrise came close.

But when at last he turned back into the room, he saw that he was no longer alone. Crouching against the opposite wall there was a hooded figure steadily watching him.

VI

His Companion in Prison

S hocks of terror, as they increase in number, apparently lessen in effect; the repeated calls made upon Jimbo's soul by the emotions of fear and astonishment had numbed it; otherwise the knowledge that he was locked in the room with this mysterious creature beyond all possibility of escape must have frightened him, as the saying is, out of his skin.

As it was, however, he kept his head in a wonderful manner, and simply stared at the silent intruder as hard as ever he could stare. How in the world it got in was the principal thought in his mind, and after that: what in the world was it?

The dawn must have come very swiftly, or else he had been staring longer than he knew, for just then the sun topped the edge of the world and the window-sill simultaneously, and sent a welcome ray of sunshine into the dingy room. It turned the grey light to silver, and fell full upon the huddled figure crouching against the opposite wall. Jimbo caught his breath, and stared harder than ever.

It was a human figure, the figure, apparently, of a man, sitting crumpled up in a very uncomfortable sort of position on his haunches. It sat perfectly still. A black cloak, with loose sleeves, and a cowl or hood that completely concealed the face, covered it from head to foot. The material of the cloak could not have been very thick, for inside the hood he caught the gleam of eyes as they roamed about the room and followed his movements. But for this glitter of the moving eyes it might have been a figure carved in wood. Was it going to sit there for ever watching him? At first he was afraid it was going to speak; then he was afraid it wasn't. It might rise suddenly and come towards him; yet the thought that it would not move at all was worse still.

In this way the two faced each other for several minutes until, just as the position was becoming simply unbearable, a low whisper ran round the room: "At last! Oh! I've found him at last!" Jimbo was not quite sure of the words, though it was certainly a human voice that had spoken; but, the suspense once broken, the boy could not stand it any longer, and with a rush of desperate courage he found his voice—a very husky one—and moved a step forward.

"Who are you, please, and how *did* you get in?" he ventured with a great effort.

Then he fell back against the wall, amazed at his own daring, and waited with tightly-clenched fists for an answer. But he had not to wait very long, for almost immediately the figure rose awkwardly to its feet, and came over to where he stood. Its manner of moving may best be described as shuffling; and it stretched in front of it a long cloaked arm, on which the sleeve hung, he thought, like clothes on a washing line.

He breathed hard, and waited. Like many other people with strong wills and sensitive nerves, Jimbo was both brave and a coward: he hoped nothing horrid was going to happen, but he was quite ready if it should. Yet, now that the actual moment had come, he had no particular fear, and when he felt the touch of the hand on his shoulder, the words sprang naturally to his lips with a little trembling laugh, more of wonder perhaps than anything else.

"You do look a horrid. . . *brute*," he was going to say, but at the last moment he changed it to "*thing*," for, with the true intuition of a child, he recognised that the creature inside the cloak was a kind creature and well disposed towards him. "But how did you get in?" he added, looking up bravely into the black visage, "because the doors are both locked on the outside, and I couldn't get out?"

By way of reply the figure shuffled to one side, and, taking the hand from his shoulder, pointed silently to a trap-door in the floor behind him. As he looked, he saw it was being shut down stealthily by some one beneath.

"Hush!" whispered the figure, almost inaudibly. "He's watching!"

"Who's watching?" he cried, curiosity taking the place of every other emotion. "I want to see." He ran forward to the spot where the trap-door now lay flush with the floor, but, before he had gone two steps, the black arms shot out and caught him. He turned, struggling, and in the scuffle that followed the cloak shrouding the figure became disarranged; the hood dropped from the face, and he found himself looking straight into the eyes, not of a man, but of a woman!

"It's you!" he cried, "You—!"

A shock ran right through his body from his head to his feet, like a current of electricity, and he caught his breath as though he had been struck. For one brief instant the sinister face of some one who had terrified him in the past came back vividly to his mind, and he shrank away in terror. But it was only for an instant, the twentieth part of an instant. Immediately, before he could even remember the name, recognition passed into darkness and his memory shut down with a snap. He was staring into the face of an utter stranger, about whom he knew nothing and had no feelings particularly one way or another.

"I thought I knew you," he gasped, "but I've forgotten you again—and I thought you were going to be a man, too."

"Jimbo!" cried the other, and in her voice was such unmistakable tenderness and yearning that the boy knew at once beyond doubt that she was his friend, "Jimbo!"

She knelt down on the floor beside him, so that her face was on a level with his, and then opened both her arms to him. But though Jimbo was glad to have found a friend who was going to help him, he felt no particular desire to be embraced, and he stood obstinately where he was with his back to the window.

The morning sunshine fell upon her features and touched the thick coils of her hair with glory. It was not, strictly speaking, a pretty face, but the look of real human tenderness there was very welcome and comforting, and in the kind brown eyes there shone a strange light that was not merely the reflection of the sunlight. The boy felt his heart warm to her as he looked, but her expression puzzled him, and he would not accept the invitation of her arms.

"Won't you come to me?" she said, her arms still outstretched.

"I want to know who you are, and what I'm doing here," he said. "I feel so funny—so old and so young—and all mixed up. I can't make out who I am a bit. What's that funny name you call me?"

"Jimbo is your name," she said softly.

"Then what's *your* name?" he asked quickly.

"My name," she repeated slowly after a pause, "is not—as nice as yours. Besides, you need not know my name—you might dislike it."

"But I must have something to call you," he persisted.

"But if I told you, and you disliked the name, you might dislike *me* too," she said, still hesitating.

Jimbo saw the expression of sadness in her eyes, and it won his confidence though he hardly knew why. He came up closer to her and put his puzzled little face next to hers.

"I like you very much already," he whispered, "and if your name is a horrid one I'll change it for you at once. Please tell me what it is."

She drew the boy to her and gave him a little hug, and he did not resist. For a long time she did not answer. He felt vaguely that

　　　　　　　　　　　　　　　ALGERNON BLACKWOOD

something of dreadful importance hung about this revelation of her name. He repeated his question, and at length she replied, speaking in a very low voice, and with her eyes fixed intently upon his face.

"My name," she said, "is Ethel Lake."

"Ethel Lake," he repeated after her. The words sounded somehow familiar to him; surely he had heard that name before. Were not the words associated with something in his past that had been unpleasant? A curious sinking sensation came over him as he heard them.

His companion watched him intently while he repeated the words over to himself several times, as if to make sure he had got them right. There was a moment's hesitation as he slowly went over them once again. Then he turned to her, laughing.

"I like your name, Ethel Lake," he said. "It's a nice name—Miss— Miss—" Again he hesitated, while a little warning tremor ran through his mind, and he wondered for an instant why he said "Miss." But it passed as suddenly as it had come, and he finished the sentence—"Miss Lake, I shall call you." He stared into her eyes as he said it.

"Then you don't remember me at all?" she cried, with a sigh of intense relief. "You've quite forgotten?"

"I never saw you before, did I? How can I remember you? I don't remember any of the things I've forgotten. Are you one of them?"

For reply she caught him to her breast and kissed him. "You precious little boy!" she said. "I'm so glad, oh, so glad!"

"But do you remember *me*?" he asked, sorely puzzled. "Who am I? Haven't I been born yet, or something funny like that?"

"If you don't remember *me*," said the other, her face happy with smiles that had evidently come only just in time to prevent tears, "there's not much good telling you who *you* are. But your name, if you really want to know, is—" She hesitated a moment.

"Be quick, Eth—Miss Lake, or you'll forget it again."

She laughed rather bitterly. "Oh, I never forget. I can't!" she said. "I wish I could. Your name is James Stone, and Jimbo is 'short' for James. Now you know."

She might just as well have said Bill Sykes for all the boy knew or remembered.

"What a silly name!" he laughed. "But it can't be my real name, or I should know it. I never heard it before." After a moment he added, "Am I an old man? I feel just like one. I suppose I'm grown up—grown up so fast that I've forgotten what came before—"

"You're not grown up, dear, at least, not exactly—" She glanced down at his alpaca knickerbockers and brown stockings; and as he followed her eyes and saw the dirty buttoned-boots there came into his mind some dim memory of where he had last put them on, and of some one who had helped him. But it all passed like a swift meteor across the dark night of his forgetfulness and was lost in mist.

"You mustn't judge by these silly clothes," he laughed. "I shall change them as soon as I get—as soon as I can find—" He stopped short. No words came. A feeling of utter loneliness and despair swept suddenly over him, drenching him from head to foot. He felt lost and friendless, naked, homeless, cold. He was ever on the brink of regaining a whole lot of knowledge and experience that he had known once long ago, ever so long ago, but it always kept just out of his reach. He glanced at Miss Lake, feeling that she was his only possible comfort in a terrible situation. She met his look and drew him tenderly towards her.

"Now, listen to me," she said gently, "I've something to tell you—about myself."

He was all attention in a minute.

"I am a discharged governess," she began, holding her breath when once the words were out.

"Discharged!" he repeated vaguely. "What's that? What for?"

"For frightening a child. I told a little boy awful stories that weren't true. They terrified him so much that I was sent away. That's why I'm here now. It's my punishment. I am a prisoner here until I can find him—and help him to escape—"

"Oh, I say!" he exclaimed quickly, as though remembering something. But it passed, and he looked up at her half-bored, half-politely. "Escape from what?" he asked.

"From here. This is the Empty House I told the stories about; *and you are the little boy I frightened*. Now, at last, I've found you, and am going to save you." She paused, watching him with eyes that never left his face for an instant.

Jimbo was delighted to hear he was going to be rescued, but he felt no interest at all in her story of having frightened a little boy, who was himself. He thought it was very nice of her to take so much trouble, and he told her so, and when he went up and kissed her and thanked her, he saw to his surprise that she was crying. For the life of him he could not understand why a discharged governess whom he met, apparently, for the first time in the Empty House, should weep over him and show him so much affection. But he could think of nothing to say, so he just waited till she had finished.

"You see, if I can save you," she said between her sobs, "it will be all right again, and I shall be forgiven, and shall be able to escape with you. I want you to escape, so that you can get back to life again."

"Oh, then I'm dead, am I?"

"Not exactly dead," she said, drying her eyes with the corner of her black hood. "You've had a funny accident, you know. If your body gets all right, so that you can go back and live in it again, then you're not dead. But if it's so badly injured that you can't work in it any more, then you are dead, and will have to stay dead. You're still joined to the body in a fashion, you see."

He stared and listened, not understanding much. It all bored him. She talked without explaining, he thought. An immense sponge had passed over the slate of the past and wiped it clean beyond recall. He was utterly perplexed.

"How funny you are!" he said vaguely, thinking more of her tears than her explanations.

"Water won't stay in a cracked bottle," she went on, "and you can't stay in a broken body. But they're trying to mend it now, and if we can escape in time you can be an ordinary, happy little boy in the world again."

"Then are you dead, too?" he asked, "or nearly dead?"

"I am out of my body, like you," she answered evasively, after a moment's pause.

He was still looking at her in a dazed sort of way, when she suddenly sprang to her feet and let the hood drop back over her face.

"Hush!" she whispered, "he's listening again."

At the same moment a sound came from beneath the floor on the other side of the room, and Jimbo saw the trap-door being slowly raised above the level of the floor.

"Your number is 102," said a voice that sounded like the rushing of a river.

Instantly the trap-door dropped again, and he heard heavy steps rumbling away into the interior of the house. He looked at his companion and saw her terrified face as she lifted her hood.

"He always blunders along like that," she whispered, bending her head on one side to listen. "He can't see properly in the daylight. He hates sunshine, and usually only goes out after dark." She was white and trembling.

"Is that the person who brought me in here this morning at such a frightful pace?" he asked, bewildered.

She nodded. "He wanted to get in before it was light, so that you couldn't see his face."

"Is he such a fright?" asked the boy, beginning to share her evident feeling of horror.

"He *is* Fright!" she said in an awed whisper. "But never talk about him again unless you can't help it; he always knows when he's being talked about, and he likes it, because it gives him more power."

Jimbo only stared at her without comprehending. Then his mind jumped to something else he wanted badly to have explained, and he asked her about his number, and why he was called No. 102.

"Oh, that's easier," she said, "102 is your number among the Frightened Children; there are 101 of them, and you are the last arrival. Haven't you seen them yet? It is also the temperature of your broken little body lying on the bed in the night nursery at home," she added, though he hardly caught her words, so low were they spoken.

Jimbo then described how the children had sung and danced to him, and went on to ask a hundred questions about them. But Miss Lake would give him very little information, and said he would not have very much to do with them. Most of them had been in the House for years and years—so long that they could probably never escape at all.

"They are all frightened children," she said. "Little ones scared out of their wits by silly people who meant to amuse them with stories, or to frighten them into being well behaved—nursery-maids, elder sisters, and even governesses!"

"And they can never escape?"

"Not unless the people who frightened them come to their rescue and *run the risk of being caught themselves*."

As she spoke there rose from the depths of the house the sound of muffled voices, children's voices singing faintly together; it rose and fell exactly like the wind, and with as little tune; it was weird and magical, but so utterly mournful that the boy felt the tears start to his eyes. It drifted away, too, just as the wind does over the tops of the trees, dying into the distance; and all became still again.

"It's just like the wind," he said, "and I do love the wind. It makes me feel so sad and so happy. Why is it?"

The governess did not answer.

"How old am I *really*?" he went on. "How can I be so old and so ignorant? I've forgotten such an awful lot of knowledge."

"The fact is—well, perhaps, you won't quite understand—but you're really two ages at once. Sometimes you feel as old as your body, and sometimes as old as your soul. You're still connected with your body; so you get the sensations of both mixed up."

"Then is the body younger than the soul?"

"The soul—that is yourself," she answered, "is, oh, so old, awfully old, as old as the stars, and older. But the body is no older than itself—of course, how could it be?"

"Of course," repeated the boy, who was not listening to a word she said. "How could it be?"

"But it doesn't matter how old you are or how young you feel, as long as you don't hate me for having frightened you," she said after a pause. "That's the chief thing."

He was very, very puzzled. He could not help feeling it had been rather unkind of her to frighten him so badly that he had literally been frightened out of his skin; but he couldn't remember anything about it, and she was taking so much trouble to save him now that he quite forgave her. He nestled up against her, and said of course he liked her, and she stroked his curly head and mumbled a lot of things to herself that he couldn't understand a bit.

But in spite of his new-found friend the feeling of over-mastering loneliness would suddenly rush over him. She might be a protector, but she was not a *real* companion; and he knew that somewhere or other he had left a lot of other *real* companions whom he now missed dreadfully. He longed more than he could say for freedom; he wanted to be able to come and go as he pleased; to play about in a garden somewhere as of old; to wander over soft green lawns among laburnums and sweet-smelling lilac trees, and to be up to all his old tricks and mischief—though he could not remember in detail what they were.

In a word, he wanted to escape; his whole being yearned to escape and be free again; yet here he was a wretched prisoner in a room like a prison-cell, with a sort of monster for a keeper, and a troop of horrible frightened children somewhere else in the house to keep him company. And outside there was only a hard, narrow, paved courtyard with a high wall round it. Oh, it was too terrible to think of, and his heart sank down within him till he felt as if he could do nothing else but cry.

"I shall save you in time," whispered the governess, as though she read his thoughts. "You must be patient, and do what I tell you, and I promise to get you out. Only be brave, and don't ask too many questions. We shall win in the end and escape."

Suddenly he looked up, with quite a new expression in his face. "But I say, Miss Cake, I'm frightfully hungry. I've had nothing to eat since—I can't remember when, but ever so long ago."

"You needn't call me Miss Cake, though," she laughed.

"I suppose it's because I'm so hungry."

"Then you'll call me Miss Lake when you're thirsty, perhaps," she said. "But, anyhow, I'll see what I can get you. Only, you must eat as little as possible. I want you to get very thin. What you feel is not really hunger—it's only a memory of hunger, and you'll soon get used to it."

He stared at her with a very distressful little face as she crossed the room making this new announcement; and just as she disappeared through the trap-door, only her head being visible, she added with great emphasis, "The thinner you get the better; because the thinner you are the lighter you are, and the lighter you are the easier it will be to escape. Remember, the thinner the better—the lighter the better—and don't ask a lot of questions about it."

With that the trap-door closed over her, and Jimbo was left alone with her last strange words ringing in his ears.

VII

The Spell of the Empty House

It was not long before Jimbo realised that the House, and everything connected with it, spelt for him one message, and one only—a message of fear. From the first day of his imprisonment the forces of his whole being shaped themselves without further ado into one intense, single, concentrated desire to *escape*.

Freedom, escape into the world beyond that terrible high wall, was his only object, and Miss Lake, the governess, as its symbol, was his only hope. He asked a lot of questions and listened to a lot of answers, but all he really cared about was how he was going to escape, and when. All her other explanations were tedious, and he only half-listened to them. His faith in her was absolute, his patience unbounded; she had come to save him, and he knew that before long she would accomplish her end. He felt a blind and perfect confidence. But, meanwhile, his fear of the House, and his horror for the secret Being who meant to keep him prisoner till at length he became one of the troop of Frightened Children, increased by leaps and bounds.

Presently the trap-door creaked again, and the governess reappeared; in her hand was a small white jug and a soup plate.

"Thin gruel and skim milk," she explained, pouring out a substance like paste into the soup plate, and handing him a big wooden spoon.

But Jimbo's hunger had somehow vanished.

"It wasn't real hunger," she told him, "but only a sort of memory of being hungry. They're trying to feed your broken body now in the night-nursery, and so you feel a sort of ghostly hunger here even though you're out of the body."

"It's easily satisfied, at any rate," he said, looking at the paste in the soup plate.

"No one actually eats or drinks here—"

"But I'm solid," he said, "am I not?"

"People always think they're solid everywhere," she laughed. "It's only a question of degree; solidity *here* means a different thing to solidity *there*."

"I can get thinner though, can't I?" he asked, thinking of her remark about escape being easier the lighter he grew.

She assured him there would be no difficulty about that, and after replying evasively to a lot more questions, she gathered up the dishes and once more disappeared through the trap-door.

Jimbo watched her going down the ladder into the black gulf below, and wondered greatly where she went to and what she did down there; but on these points the governess had refused to satisfy his curiosity, and every time she appeared or disappeared the atmosphere of mystery came and went with her.

As he stared, wondering, a sound suddenly made itself heard behind him, and on turning quickly round he saw to his great surprise that the door into the passage was open. This was more than he could resist, and in another minute, with mingled feelings of dread and delight, he was out in the passage.

When he was first brought to the house, two hours before, it had been too dark to see properly, but now the sun was high in the heavens, and the light still increasing. He crept cautiously to the head of the stairs and peered over into the well of the house. It was still too dark to make things out clearly; but, as he looked, he thought something moved among the shadows below, and for a moment his heart stood still with fear. A large grey face seemed to be staring up at him out of the gloom. He clutched the banisters and felt as if he hardly had strength enough in his legs to get back to the room he had just left; but almost immediately the terror passed, for he saw that the face resolved itself into the mingling of light and shadow, and the features, after all, were of his own creation. He went on slowly and stealthily down the staircase.

It was certainly an empty house. There were no carpets; the passages were cold and draughty; the paper curled from the damp walls, leaving ugly discoloured patches about; cobwebs hung in many places from the ceiling, the windows were more or less broken, and all were coated so thickly with dirt that the rain had traced little furrows from top to bottom. Shadows hung about everywhere, and Jimbo thought every minute he saw moving figures; but the figures always resolved themselves into nothing when he looked closely.

He began to wonder how far it was safe to go, and why the governess had arranged for the door to be opened—for he felt sure it was she who had done this, and that it was all right for him to come out. Fright, she had said, was never about in the daylight. But, at the same time, something warned him to be ready at a moment's notice to turn and dash up the stairs again to the room where he was at least comparatively safe.

So he moved along very quietly and very cautiously. He passed many rooms with the doors open—all empty and silent; some of them had tables and chairs, but no sign of occupation; the grates were black and empty, the walls blank, the windows unshuttered. Everywhere was only silence and shadows; there was no sign of the frightened children, or of where they lived; no trace of another staircase leading to the region where the governess went when she disappeared down the ladder through the trap-door—only hushed, listening, cold silence, and shadows that seemed for ever shifting from place to place as he moved past them. This illusion of people peering at him from corners, and behind doors just ajar, was very strong; yet whenever he turned his head to face them, lo, they were gone, and the shadows rushed in to fill their places.

The spell of the Empty House was weaving itself slowly and surely about his heart.

Yet he went on pluckily, full of a dreadful curiosity, continuing his search, and at length, after passing through another gloomy passage, he was in the act of crossing the threshold of an open door leading out into the courtyard, when he stopped short and clutched the door-posts with both hands.

Some one had laughed!

He turned, trying to look in every direction at once, but there was no sign of any living being. Yet the sound was close beside him; he could still hear it ringing in his ears—a mocking sort of laugh, in a harsh, guttural voice. The blood froze in his veins, and he hardly knew which way to turn, when another voice sounded, and his terror disappeared as if by magic.

It was Miss Lake's voice calling to him over the banisters at the top of the house, and its tone was so cheerful that all his courage came back in a twinkling.

"Go out into the yard," she called, "and play in the sunshine. But don't stay too long."

Jimbo answered "All right" in a rather feeble little voice, and went on down the passage and out into the yard.

The June sunshine lay hot and still over the paved court, and he looked up into the blue sky overhead. As he looked at the high wall that closed it in on three sides, he realised more than ever that he was caught in a monstrous trap from which there could be no ordinary means of escape. He could never climb over such a wall even with a ladder. He walked out a little way and noticed the rank weeds growing in patches in the corners; decay and neglect left everywhere their dismal signs; the yard, in spite of the sunlight, seemed as gloomy and cheerless as the house itself.

In one corner stood several little white upright stones, each about three feet high; there seemed to be some writing on them, and he was in the act of going nearer to inspect, when a window opened and he heard some one calling to him in a loud, excited whisper:

"Hst! Come in, Jimbo, at once. Quick! Run for your life!"

He glanced up, quaking with fear, and saw the governess leaning out of the open window. At another window, a little beyond her, he thought a number of white little faces pressed against the glass, but he had no time to look more closely, for something in Miss Lake's voice made him turn and run into the house and up the stairs as though Fright himself were close at his heels. He flew up the three flights, and found the governess coming out on the top landing to meet him. She caught him in her arms and dashed back into the room, as if there was not a moment to be lost, slamming the door behind her.

"How in the world did you get out?" she gasped, breathless as himself almost, and pale with alarm. "Another second and He'd have had you—!"

"I found the door open—"

"He opened it on purpose," she whispered, looking quickly round the room. "He meant you to go out."

"But you called to me to play in the yard," he said. "I heard you. So of course I thought it was safe."

"No," she declared, "I never called to you. That wasn't my voice. That was one of his tricks. I only this minute found the door open and you gone. Oh, Jimbo, that was a narrow escape; you must never go out of this room till—till I tell you. And never believe any of these voices you hear—you'll hear lots of them, saying all sorts of things—but unless you *see* me, don't believe it's my voice."

Jimbo promised. He was very frightened; but she would not tell him any more, saying it would only make it more difficult to escape if he knew too much in advance. He told her about the laugh, and the gravestones, and the faces at the other window, but she would not tell him what he wanted to know, and at last he gave up asking. A very deep impression had been made on his mind, however, and he began to realise, more than he had hitherto done, the horror of his prison and the power of his dreadful keeper.

But when he began to look about him again, he noticed that there was a new thing in the room. The governess had left him, and was bending over it. She was doing something very busily indeed. He asked her what it was.

"I'm making your bed," she said.

It was, indeed, a bed, and he felt as he looked at it that there was something very familiar and friendly about the yellow framework and the little brass knobs.

"I brought it up just now," she explained. "But it's not for sleeping in. It's only for you to lie down on, and also partly to deceive Him."

"Why not for sleeping?"

"There's no sleeping at all here," she went on calmly.

"Why not?"

"You can't sleep out of your body," she laughed.

"Why not?" he asked again.

"Your body goes to sleep, but *you* don't," she explained.

"Oh, I see." His head was whirling. "And my body—my real body—"

"Is lying asleep—unconscious they call it—in the night-nursery at home. It's sound asleep. That's why you're here. It can't wake up till you go back to it, and you can't go back to it till you escape—even if it's ready for you before then. The bed is only for you to rest on, for you can *rest* though you can't *sleep*."

Jimbo stared blankly at the governess for some minutes. He was debating something in his mind, something very important, and just then it was his Older Self, and not the child, that was uppermost. Apparently it was soon decided, for he walked sedately up to her and said very gravely, with her serious eyes fixed on his face, "Miss Lake, are you *really* Miss Lake?"

"Of course I am."

"You're not a trick of His, like the voices, I mean?"

"No, Jimbo, I am really Miss Lake, the discharged governess who frightened you." There was profound anxiety in every word.

Jimbo waited a minute, still looking steadily into her eyes. Then he put out his hand cautiously and touched her. He rose a little on tiptoe to be on a level with her face, taking a fold of her cloak in each hand.

The soul-knowledge was in his eyes just then, not the mere curiosity of the child.

"And are you—*dead*?" he asked, sinking his voice to a whisper.

For a moment the woman's eyes wavered. She turned white and tried to move away; but the boy seized her hand and peered more closely into her face.

"I mean, if we escape and I get back into my body," he whispered, "will you get back into yours too?"

The governess made no reply, and shifted uneasily on her feet. But the boy would not let her go.

"Please answer," he urged, still in a whisper.

"Jimbo, what funny questions you ask!" she said at last, in a husky voice, but trying to smile.

"But I want to know," he said. "I must know. I believe you are giving up everything just to save me—*everything*; and I don't want to be saved unless you come too. Tell me!"

The colour came back to her cheeks a little, and her eyes grew moist. Again she tried to slip past him, but he prevented her.

"You must tell me," he urged; "I would rather stay here with you than escape back into my body and leave you behind."

Jimbo knew it was his Older Self speaking—the freed spirit rather than the broken body—but he felt the strain was very great; he could not keep it up much longer; any minute he might slip back into the child again, and lose interest, and be unequal to the task he now saw so clearly before him.

"Quick!" he cried in a louder voice. "Tell me! You are giving up everything to save me, aren't you? And if I escape you will be left alone—quick, answer me! Oh, be quick, I'm slipping back—"

Already he felt his thoughts becoming confused again, as the spirit merged back into the child; in another minute the boy would usurp the older self.

"You see," began the governess at length, speaking very gently and sadly, "I am bound to make amends whatever happens. I must atone—"

But already he found it hard to follow.

"Atone," he asked, "what does '*atone*' mean?" He moved back a step, and glanced about the room. The moment of concentration had passed without bearing fruit; his thoughts began to wander again like a child's. "Anyhow, we shall escape together when the chance comes, shan't we?" he said.

ALGERNON BLACKWOOD

"Yes, darling, we shall," she said in a broken voice. "And if you do what I tell you, it will come very soon, I hope." She drew him towards her and kissed him, and though he didn't respond very heartily, he felt he liked it, and was sure that she was good, and meant to do the best possible for him.

Jimbo asked nothing more for some time; he turned to the bed where he found a mattress and a blanket, but no sheets, and sat down on the edge and waited. The governess was standing by the window looking out; her back was turned to him. He heard an occasional deep sigh come from her, but he was too busy now with his own sensations to trouble much about her. Looking past her he saw the sea of green leaves dancing lazily in the sunshine. Something seemed to beckon him from beyond the high wall, and he longed to go out and play in the shade of the elms and hawthorns; for the horror of the Empty House was closing in upon him steadily but surely, and he longed for escape into a bright, unhaunted atmosphere, more than anything else in the whole world.

His thoughts ran on and on in this vein, till presently he noticed that the governess was moving about the room. She crossed over and tried first one door and then the other; both were fastened. Next she lifted the trap-door and peered down into the black hole below. That, too, apparently was satisfactory. Then she came over to the bedside on tiptoe.

"Jimbo, I've got something very important to ask you," she began.

"All right," he said, full of curiosity.

"You must answer me very exactly. Everything depends on it."

"I will."

She took another long look round the room, and then, in a still lower whisper, bent over him, and asked:

"Have you any pain?"

"Where?" he asked, remembering to be exact.

"Anywhere."

He thought a moment.

"None, thank you."

"None at all—anywhere?" she insisted.

"None at all—anywhere," he said with decision.

She seemed disappointed.

"Never mind; it's a little soon yet, perhaps," she said. "We must have patience. It will come in time."

"But I don't want any pain," he said, rather ruefully.

"You can't escape till it comes."

"I don't understand a bit what you mean." He began to feel alarmed at the notion of escape and pain going together.

"You'll understand later, though," she said soothingly, "and it won't hurt *very* much. The sooner the pain comes, the sooner we can try to escape. Nowhere can there be escape without it."

And with that she left him, disappearing without another word into the hole below the trap, and leaving him, disconsolate yet excited, alone in the room.

VIII

The Gallery of Ancient Memories

With every one, of course, the measurement of time depends largely upon the state of the emotions, but in Jimbo's case it was curiously exaggerated. This may have been because he had no standard of memory by which to test the succession of minutes; but, whatever it was, the hours passed very quickly, and the evening shadows were already darkening the room when at length he got up from the mattress and went over to the window.

Outside the high elms were growing dim; soon the stars would be out in the sky. The afternoon had passed away like magic, and the governess still left him alone; he could not quite understand why she went away for such long periods.

The darkness came down very swiftly, and it was night almost before he knew it. Yet he felt no drowsiness, no desire to yawn and get under sheets and blankets; sleep was evidently out of the question, and the hours slipped away so rapidly that it made little difference whether he sat up all night or whether he slept.

It was his first night in the Empty House, and he wondered how many more he would spend there before escape came. He stood at the window, peering out into the growing darkness and thinking long, long thoughts. Below him yawned the black gulf of the yard, and the outline of the enclosing wall was only just visible, but beyond the elms rose far into the sky, and he could hear the wind singing softly in their branches. The sound was very sweet; it suggested freedom, and the flight of birds, and all that was wild and unrestrained. The wind could never really be a prisoner; its voice sang of open spaces and unbounded distances, of flying clouds and mountains, of mighty woods and dancing waves; above all, of wings—free, swift, and unconquerable wings.

But this rushing song of wind among the leaves made him feel too sad to listen long, and he lay down upon the bed again, still thinking, thinking.

The house was utterly still. Not a thing stirred within its walls. He felt lonely, and began to long for the companionship of the governess; he would have called aloud for her to come only he was afraid to break the appalling silence. He wondered where she was all this time and how she spent the long, dark hours of the sleepless nights. Were all these things really true that she told him? Was he actually out of his body, and was his name really Jimbo? His thoughts kept groping backwards, ever seeking the other companions he had lost; but, like a piece of stretched elastic too short to reach its object, they always came back with a snap just when he seemed on the point of finding them. He wanted these companions very badly indeed, but the struggling of his memory was painful, and he could not keep the effort up for very long at one time.

The effort once relaxed, however, his thoughts wandered freely where they would; and there rose before his mind's eye dim suggestions of memories far more distant—ghostly scenes and faces that passed before him in endless succession, but always faded away before he could properly seize and name them.

This memory, so stubborn as regards quite recent events, began to play strange tricks with him. It carried him away into a Past so remote that he could not connect it with himself at all, and it was like dreaming of scenes and events that had happened to some one else; yet, all the time, he knew quite well those things had happened to him, and to none else. It was the memory of the soul asserting itself now that the clamour of the body was low. It was an underground river coming to the surface, for odd minutes, here and there, showing its waters to the stars just long enough to catch their ghostly reflections before it rolled away underground again.

Yet, swift and transitory as they were, these glimpses brought in their train sensations that were too powerful ever to have troubled his child-mind in its present body. They stirred in him the strong emotions, the ecstasies, the terrors, the yearnings of a much more distant past; whispering to him, could he but have understood, of an infinitely deeper layer of memories and experiences which, now released from the burden of the immediate years, strove to awaken into life again. The soul in that little body covered with alpaca knickerbockers and a sailor blouse seemed suddenly to have access to a storehouse of knowledge that must have taken centuries, rather than a few short years, to acquire.

It was all very queer. The feeling of tremendous age grew mysteriously over him. He realised that he had been wandering for ages. He had been to the stars and also to the deeps; he had roamed over strange mountains far away from cities or inhabited places of the earth, and had lived by streams whose waves were silvered by moonlight dropping softly through whispering palm branches. . .

Some of these ghostly memories brought him sensations of keenest happiness—icy, silver, radiant; others swept through his heart like a cold wave, leaving behind a feeling of unutterable woe, and a sense of loneliness that almost made him cry aloud. And there came Voices too—Voices that had slept so long in the inner kingdoms of silence that they failed to rouse in him the very slightest emotion of recognition. . .

Worn out at length with the surging of these strange hosts through him, he got up and went to the open window again. The night was very dark and warm, but the stars had disappeared, and there was the hush and the faint odour of coming rain in the air. He smelt leaves and the earth and the moist things of the ground, the wonderful perfume of the life of the soil.

The wind had dropped; all was silent as the grave; the leaves of the elm trees were motionless; no bird or insect raised its voice; everything slept; he alone was watchful, awake. Leaning over the window-sill, his thoughts searched for the governess, and he wondered anew where she was spending the dark hours. She, too, he felt sure, was wakeful somewhere, watching with him, plotting their escape together, and always mindful of his safety. . .

His reverie was suddenly interrupted by the flight of an immense night-bird dropping through the air just above his head. He sprang back into the room with a startled cry, as it rushed past in the darkness with a great swishing of wings. The size of the creature filled him with awe; it was so close that the wind it made lifted the hair on his forehead, and he could almost feel the feathers brush his cheeks. He strained his eyes to try and follow it, but the shadows were too deep and he could see nothing; only in the distance, growing every moment fainter, he could hear the noise of big wings threshing the air. He waited a little, wondering if another bird would follow it, or if it would presently return to its perch on the roof; and then his thoughts passed on to uncertain memories of other big birds—hawks, owls, eagles—that he had seen somewhere in places now beyond the reach of distinct recollections. . .

Soon the light began to dawn in the east, and he made out the shape of the elm trees and the dreadful prison wall; and with the first real touch of morning light he heard a familiar creaking sound in the room behind him, and saw the black hood of the governess rising through the trap-door in the floor.

"But you've left me alone all night!" he said at once reproachfully, as she kissed him.

"On purpose," she answered. "He'd get suspicious if I stayed too much with you. It's different in the daytime, when he can't see properly."

"Where's he been all night, then?" asked the boy.

"Last night he was out most of the time—hunting—"

"Hunting!" he repeated, with excitement. "Hunting what?"

"Children—frightened children," she replied, lowering her voice. "That's how he found you."

It was a horrible thought—Fright hunting for victims to bring to his dreadful prison—and Jimbo shivered as he heard it.

"And how did you get on all this time?" she asked, hurriedly changing the subject.

"I've been remembering, that is half-remembering, an awful lot of things, and feeling, oh, so old. I never want to remember anything again," he said wearily.

"You'll forget quick enough when you get back into your body, and have only the body-memories," she said, with a sigh that he did not understand. "But, now tell me," she added, in a more serious voice, "have you had any pain yet?"

He shook his head. She stepped up beside him.

"None *there*?" she asked, touching him lightly just behind the shoulder blades.

Jimbo jumped as if he had been shot, and uttered a piercing yell.

"That hurts!" he screamed.

"I'm so glad," cried the governess. "That's the pains coming at last." Her face was beaming.

"Coming!" he echoed, "I think they've *come*. But if they hurt as much as that, I think I'd rather not escape," he added ruefully.

"The pain won't last more than a minute," she said calmly. "You must be brave and stand it. There's no escape without pain—from anything."

"If there's no other way," he said pluckily, "I'll try,—but—"

"You see," she went on, rather absently, "at this very moment the doctor is probing the wounds in your back where the horns went in—"

But he was not listening. Her explanations always made him want either to cry or to laugh. This time he laughed, and the governess joined him, while they sat on the edge of the bed together talking of many things. He did not understand all her explanations, but it comforted

ALGERNON BLACKWOOD

him to hear them. So long as somebody understood, no matter who, he felt it was all right.

In this way several days and nights passed quickly away. The pains were apparently no nearer, but as Miss Lake showed no particular anxiety about their non-arrival, he waited patiently too, dreading the moment, yet also looking forward to it exceedingly.

During the day the governess spent most of the time in the room with him; but at night, when he was alone, the darkness became enchanted, the room haunted, and he passed into the long, long Gallery of Ancient Memories.

IX

The Means of Escape

A week passed, and Jimbo began to wonder if the pains he so much dreaded, yet so eagerly longed for, were ever coming at all. The imprisonment was telling upon him, and he grew very thin, and consequently very light.

The nights, though he spent them alone, were easily borne, for he was then intensely occupied, and the time passed swiftly; the moment it was dark he stepped into the Gallery of Memories, and in a little while passed into a new world of wonder and delight. But the daytime seemed always long. He stood for hours by the window watching the trees and the sky, and what he saw always set painful currents running through his blood—unsatisfied longings, yearnings, and immense desires he never could understand.

The white clouds on their swift journeys took with them something from his heart every time he looked upon them; they melted into air and blue sky, and lo! that "something" came back to him charged with all the wild freedom and magic of open spaces, distance, and rushing winds.

But the change was close at hand.

One night, as he was standing by the open window listening to the drip of the rain, he felt a deadly weakness steal over him; the strength went out of his legs. First he turned hot, and then he turned cold; clammy perspiration broke out all over him, and it was all he could do to crawl across the room and throw himself on to the bed. But no sooner was he stretched out on the mattress than the feelings passed entirely, and left behind them an intoxicating sense of strength and lightness. His muscles became like steel springs; his bones were strong as iron and light as cork; a wonderful vigour had suddenly come into him, and he felt as if he had just stepped from a dungeon into fresh air. He was ready to face anything in the world.

But, before he had time to realise the full enjoyment of these new sensations, a stinging, blinding pain shot suddenly through his right shoulder as if a red-hot iron had pierced to the very bone. He screamed out in agony; though, even while he screamed, the pain passed. Then the same thing happened in his other shoulder. It shot through his back with equal swiftness, and was gone, leaving him lying on the bed trembling with pain. But the instant it was gone the delightful sensations of strength and lightness returned, and he felt as if his whole body were charged with some new and potent force.

The pains had come at last! Jimbo had no notion how they could possibly be connected with escape, but Miss Lake—his kind and faithful friend, Miss Lake—had said that no escape was possible without them; and had promised that they should be brief. And this was true, for the entire episode had not taken a minute of time.

"Escape, Escape!"—the words rushed through him like a flame of fire. Out of this dreadful Empty House, into the open spaces; beyond the prison wall; out where the wind and the rain could touch him; where he could feel the grass beneath his feet, and could see the whole sky at once, instead of this narrow strip through the window. His thoughts flew to the stars and the clouds. . .

But a strange humming of voices interrupted his flight of imagination, and he saw that the room was suddenly full of moving figures. They were passing before him with silent footsteps, across the window from door to door. How they had come in, or how they went out, he never knew; but his heart stood still for an instant as he recognised the mournful figures of the Frightened Children filing before him in a slow procession. They were singing—though it sounded more like a chorus of whispering than actual singing—and as they moved past with the measured steps of their sorrowful dance, he caught the words of the song he had heard them sing when he first came into the house:—

> *"We hear the little voices in the wind*
> *Singing of freedom we may never find."*

Jimbo put his fingers into his ears, but still the sound came through. He heard the words almost as if they were inside himself—his own thoughts singing:—

> *"We hear the little footsteps in the rain*
> *Running to help us, though they run in vain,*
> *Tapping in hundreds on the window-pane."*

The horrible procession filed past and melted away near the door. They were gone as mysteriously as they had come, and almost before he realised it.

He sprang from the bed and tried the doors; both were locked. How in the world had the children got in and out? The whispering voices rose again on the night air, and this time he was sure they came from outside. He ran to the open window and thrust his head out cautiously. Sure enough, the procession was moving slowly, still with the steps of that impish dance across the courtyard stones. He could just make out the slow waving arms, the thin bodies, and the white little faces as they passed on silent feet through the darkness, and again a fragment of the song rose to his ears as he watched, and filled him with an overpowering sadness:—

> *"We have no joy in any children's game,*
> *For happiness to us is but a name,*
> *Since Terror kissed us with his lips of flame."*

Then he noticed that the group was growing smaller. Already the numbers were less. Somewhere, over there in the dark corner of the yard, the children disappeared, though it was too dark to see precisely how or where.

"We dance with phantoms, and with shadows play," rose to his ears.

Suddenly he remembered the little white upright stones he had seen in that corner of the yard, and understood. One by one they vanished just behind those stones.

Jimbo shivered, and drew his head in. He did not like those upright stones; they made him uncomfortable and afraid. Now, however, the last child had disappeared and the song had ceased. He realised what his fate would be if the escape were not successful; he would become one of this band of Frightened Children; dwelling somewhere behind the upright stones; a terrified shadow, waiting in vain to be rescued, waiting perhaps for ever and ever. The thought brought the tears to his eyes, but he somehow managed to choke them down. He knew it was the young portion of him only that felt afraid—the body; the older self could not feel fear, and had nothing to do with tears.

He lay down again upon the hard mattress and waited; and soon afterwards the first crimson streaks of sunrise appeared behind the

ALGERNON BLACKWOOD

high elms, and rooks began to caw and shake their wings in the upper branches. A little later the governess came in.

Before he could move out of the way—for he disliked being embraced—she had her arms round his neck, and was covering him with kisses. He saw tears in her eyes.

"You darling Jimbo!" she cried, "they've come at last."

"How do you know?" he asked, surprised at her knowledge and puzzled by her display of emotion.

"I heard you scream to begin with. Besides, I've been watching."

"Watching?"

"Yes, and listening too, every night, every single night. You've hardly been a minute out of my sight," she added.

"I think it's awfully good of you," he said doubtfully, "but—"

A flood of questions followed—about the upright stones, the shadowy children, where she spent the night "watching him," and a hundred other things besides. But he got little satisfaction out of her. He never did when it was Jimbo, the child, that asked; and he remained Jimbo, the child, all that day. She only told him that all was going well. The pains had come; he had grown nice and thin, and light; the children had come into his room as a hint that he belonged to their band, and other things had happened about which she would tell him later. The crisis was close at hand. That was all he could get out of her.

"It won't be long now," she said excitedly. "They'll come tonight, I expect."

"What will come tonight?" he asked, with querulous wonder.

"Wait and see!" was all the answer he got. "Wait and see!"

She told him to lie quietly on the bed and to have patience.

With asking questions, and thinking, and wondering, the day passed very quickly. With the lengthening shadows his excitement began to grow. Presently Miss Lake took her departure and went off to her unknown and mysterious abode; he watched her disappear through the floor with mingled feelings, wondering what would have happened before he saw her again. She gave him a long, last look as she sank away below the boards, but it was a look that brought him fresh courage, and her eyes were happy and smiling.

Tingling already with expectancy he got into the bed and lay down, his brain alive with one word—ESCAPE.

From where he lay he saw the stars in the narrow strip of sky; he heard the wind whispering in the branches; he even smelt the perfume of the fields and hedges—grass, flowers, dew, and the sweet earth—the odours of freedom.

The governess had, for some reason she refused to explain, taken his blouse away with her. For a long time he puzzled over this, seeking reasons and finding none. But, while in the act of stroking his bare arms, the pains of the night before suddenly returned to both shoulders at once. Fire seemed to run down his back, splitting his bones apart, and then passed even more quickly than before, leaving him with the same wonderful sensations of lightness and strength. He felt inclined to shout and run and jump, and it was only the memory of the governess's earnest caution to "lie quietly" that prevented his new emotions passing into acts.

With very great effort he lay still all night long; and it was only when the room at last began to get light again that he turned on his side, preparatory to getting up.

But there was something new—something different! He rested on his elbow, waiting. Something had happened to him. Cautiously he sat on the edge of the bed, and stretched out one foot and touched the floor. Excitement ran through him like a wave. There was a great change, a tremendous change; for as he stepped out gingerly on to the floor *something followed him from the bed*. It clung to his back; it touched both shoulders at once; it stroked his ribs, and tickled the skin of his arms.

Half frightened, he brought the other leg over, and stood boldly upright on both feet. But the weight still clung to his back. He looked over his shoulder. Yes! it was trailing after him from the bed; it was fan-shaped, and brilliant in colour. He put out a hand and touched it; it was soft and glossy; then he took it deliberately between his fingers; it was smooth as velvet, and had numerous tiny ribs running along it.

Seizing it at last with all his courage, he pulled it forward in front of him for a better view, only to discover that it would not come out beyond a certain distance, and seemed to have got caught somehow between his shoulders—just where the pains had been. A second pull, more vigorous than the first, showed that it was not caught, but *fastened* to his skin; it divided itself, moreover, into two portions, one half coming from each shoulder.

"I do believe they're feathers!" he exclaimed, his eyes almost popping out of his head.

Then, with a sudden flash of comprehension, he saw it all, and understood. They were, indeed, feathers; but they were something more than feathers merely. *They were wings!*

ALGERNON BLACKWOOD

Jimbo caught his breath and stared in silence. He felt dazed. Then bit by bit the fragments of the weird mosaic fell into their proper places, and he began to understand. Escape was to be by flight. It filled him with such a whirlwind of delight and excitement that he could scarcely keep from screaming aloud.

Lost in wonder, he took a step forward, and watched with bulging eyes how the wings followed him, their tips trailing along the floor. They were a beautiful deep red, and hung down close and warm beside his body; glossy, sleek, magical. And when, later, the sun burst into the room and turned their colour into living flame, he could not resist the temptation to kiss them. He seized them, and rubbed their soft surfaces over his face. Such colours he had never seen before, and he wanted to be sure that they really belonged to him and were intended for actual use.

Slowly, without using his hands, he raised them into the air. The effort was a perfectly easy muscular effort from the shoulders that came naturally, though he did not quite understand how he accomplished it. The wings rose in a fine, graceful sweep, curving over his head till the tips of the feathers met, touching the walls as they rose, and almost reaching to the ceiling.

He gave a howl of delight, for this sight was more than he could manage without some outlet for his pent-up emotion; and at the same moment the trap-door shot open, and the governess came into the room with such a bang and a clatter that Jimbo knew at once her excitement was as great as his own. In her hands she carried the blouse she had taken away the night before. She held it out to him without a word. Her eyes were shining like electric lamps. In less than a second he had slipped his wings through the neatly-made slits, but before he could practise them again, Miss Lake rushed over to him, her face radiant with happiness.

"Jimbo! My darling Jimbo!" she cried—and then stopped short, apparently unable to express her emotion.

The next instant he was enveloped, wings and all, in a warm confusion of kisses, congratulations and folds of hood.

When they became disentangled again the governess went down on her knees and made a careful examination; she pulled the wings out to their full extent and found that they stretched about four feet and a half from tip to tip.

"They *are* beauties!" she exclaimed enthusiastically, "and full grown and strong. I'm not surprised they took so long coming."

"Long!" he echoed, "I thought they came awfully quickly."

"Not half so quickly as they'll go," she interrupted; adding, when she saw his expression of dismay, "I mean, you'll fly like the wind with them."

Jimbo was simply breathless with excitement. He wanted to jump out of the window and escape at once. The blue sky and the sunshine and the white flying clouds sent him an irresistible invitation. He could not wait a minute longer.

"Quick," he cried, "I can't wait! They may go again. Show me how to use them. Oh! do show me."

"I'll show you everything in time," she answered. There was something in her voice that made him pause in his excitement. He looked at her in silence for some minutes.

"But how are *you* going to escape?" he asked at length. "You haven't got"—he stopped short.

The governess stepped back a few paces from him. She threw back the hood from her face. Then she lifted the long black cloak that hung like a cassock almost to her ankles and had always enveloped her hitherto.

Jimbo stared. Falling from her shoulders, and folding over her hips, he saw long red feathers clinging to her; and when he dashed forward to touch them with his hands, he found they were just as sleek and smooth and glossy as his own.

"And you never told me all this time?" he gasped.

"It was safer not," she said. "You'd have been stroking and feeling your shoulders the whole time, and the wings might never have come at all."

She spread out her wings as she spoke to their full extent; they were nearly six feet across, and the deep crimson on the under side was so exquisite, gleaming in the sunlight, that Jimbo ran in and nestled beneath the feathers, tickling his cheeks with the fluffy surface and running his fingers with childish delight along the slender red quills.

"You precious child," she said, tenderly folding her wings round him and kissing the top of his head. "Always remember that I really love you; no matter what happens, remember that, and I'll save you."

"And we shall escape together?" he asked, submitting for once to the caresses with a good grace.

"We shall escape from the Empty House together," she replied evasively. "How far we can go after that depends—on you."

"On me?"

"If you love me enough—as I love you, Jimbo—we can never separate

ALGERNON BLACKWOOD

again, because love ties us together for ever. Only," she added, "it must be mutual."

"I love you very much," he said, puzzled a little. "Of course I do."

"If you've really forgiven me for being the cause of your coming here," she said, "we can always be together, but—"

"I don't remember, but I've forgiven you—that *other you*—long ago," he said simply. "If you hadn't brought me here, I should never have met you."

"That's not real forgiveness—quite," she sighed, half to herself.

But Jimbo could not follow this sort of conversation for long; he was too anxious to try his wings for one thing.

"Is it *very* difficult to use them?" he asked.

"Try," she said.

He stood in the centre of the floor and raised them again and again. They swept up easily, meeting over his head, and the air whistled musically through them. Evidently, they had their proper muscles, for it was no great effort, and when he folded them again by his side they fell into natural curves over his arms as if they had been there all his life. The sound of the feathers threshing the air filled him with delight and made him think of the big night-bird that had flown past the window during the night. He told the governess about it, and she burst out laughing.

"I was that big bird!" she said.

"You!"

"I perched on the roof every night to watch over you. I flew down that time because I was afraid you were trying to climb out of the window."

This was indeed a proof of devotion, and Jimbo felt that he could never doubt her again; and when she went on to tell him about his wings and how to use them he listened with his very best attention and tried hard to learn and understand.

"The great difficulty is that you can't practise properly," she explained. "There's no room in here, and yet you can't get out till you *fly* out. It's the first swoop that decides all. You have to drop straight out of this window, and if you use the wings properly they will carry you in a single swoop over the wall and right up into the sky."

"But if I miss—?"

"You can't miss," she said with decision, "but, if you did, you would be a prisoner here for ever. HE would catch you in the yard and tear your wings off. It is just as well that you should know this at once."

Jimbo shuddered as he heard her.

"When can we try?" he asked anxiously.

"Very soon now. The muscles must harden first, and that takes a little time. You must practise flapping your wings until you can do it easily four hundred times a minute. When you can do that it will be time for the first start. You must keep your head steady and not get giddy; the novelty of the motion—the ground rushing up into your face and the whistling of the wind—are apt to confuse at first, but it soon passes, and you must have confidence. I can only help you up to a certain point; the rest depends on you."

"And the first jump?"

"You'll have to make that by yourself," she said; "but you'll do it all right. You're very light, and won't go too near the ground. You see, we're like bats, and cannot rise from the earth. We can only fly by dropping from a height, and that's what makes the first plunge rather trying. But you won't fall," she added, "and remember, I shall always be within reach."

"You're awfully kind to me," said Jimbo, feeling his little soul more than ever invaded by the force of her unselfish care. "I promise you I'll do my best." He climbed on to her knee and stared into her anxious face.

"Then you are beginning to love me a little, aren't you?" she asked softly, putting her arms round him.

"Yes," he said decidedly. "I love you very much already."

Four hundred times a minute sounded a very great deal of wing-flapping; but Jimbo practised eagerly, and though at first he could only manage about twice a second, or one hundred and twenty times a minute, he found this increased very soon to a great deal more, and before long he was able to do the full four hundred, though only for a few minutes at a time.

He stuck to it pluckily, getting stronger every day. The governess encouraged him as much as possible, but there was very little room for her while he was at work, and he found the best way to practise was at night when she was out of the way. She told him that a large bird moved its wings about four times a second, two up-strokes and two down-strokes; but a small bird like a partridge moved its wings so rapidly it was impossible for the eye to distinguish or count the strokes. A middle course of four hundred suited his own case best, and he bent all his energies to acquire it.

He also learned that the convex outside curve of wings allowed the wind to escape over them, while the under side, being concave, held every breath. Thus the upward stroke did not simply counterbalance the downward and keep him stationary. Moreover, she showed him how the feathers underlapped each other so that the downward stroke pressed them closely together to hold the wind, whereas in the upward stroke they opened and separated, letting the air slip easily through them, thus offering less resistance to the atmosphere.

By the end of a week Jimbo had practised so hard that he could keep himself off the floor in mid-air for half an hour at a time, and even then without feeling any great fatigue. His excitement became intense; and, meanwhile, in his body on the nursery bed, though he did not know it, the fever was reaching its crisis. He could think of nothing else but the joys of flying, and what the first, awful plunge would be like, and when Miss Lake came up to him one afternoon and whispered something in his ear, he was so wildly happy that he hugged her for several minutes without the slightest coaxing.

"It's bright and clear," she explained, "and Fright will not come after us, for he fears the light, and can only fly on dark and gloomy nights."

"So we can start—?" he stammered joyfully.

"Tonight," she answered, "for our first practice-flight."

X

The Plunge

To enter the world of wings is to enter a new state of existence. The apparent loss of weight; the ability to attain full speed in a few seconds, and to stop suddenly in a headlong rush without fear of collapse; the power to steer instantly in any direction by merely changing the angle of the body; the altered and enormous view of the green world below—looking down upon forests, seas and clouds; the easy voluptuous rhythm of rising and falling in long, swinging undulations; and a hundred other things that simply defy description and can be appreciated only by actual experience, these are some of the delights of the new world of wings and flying. And the fearful joy of very high speed, especially when the exhilaration of escape is added to it, means a condition little short of real ecstasy.

Yet Jimbo's first flight, the governess had been careful to tell him, could not be the flight of final escape; for, even if the wings proved equal to a prolonged effort, escape was impossible until there was somewhere safe to escape to. So it was understood that the practice flights might be long, or might be short; the important thing, meanwhile, was to learn to fly as well as possible. For skilled flying is very different to mere headlong rushing, and both courage and perseverance are necessary to acquire it.

With rare common sense Miss Lake had said very little about the possibility of failure. Having warned him about the importance of not falling, she had then stopped, and the power of suggestion had been allowed to work only in the right direction of certain success. While the boy knew that the first plunge from the window would be a moment fraught with the highest danger, his mind only recognised the mere off-chance of falling and being caught. He felt confidence in himself, and by so much, therefore, were the chances of disaster lessened.

For the rest of the afternoon Jimbo saw nothing of his faithful companion; he spent the time practising and resting, and when weary of everything else, he went to the window and indulged in thrilling calculations about the exact height from the ground. A drop of three storeys into a paved courtyard with a monster waiting to catch him, and a high wall too close to allow a proper swing, was an alarming matter from any point of view. Fortunately, his mind dwelt more on the delight of prospective flight and freedom than on the chances of being caught.

The yard lay hot and naked in the afternoon glare and the enclosing wall had never looked more formidable; but from his lofty perch Jimbo could see beyond into soft hayfields and smiling meadows, yellow with cowslips and buttercups. Everything that flew he watched with absorbing interest: swift blackbirds, whistling as they went, and crows, their wings purple in the sunshine. The song of the larks, invisible in the sea of blue air sent a thrill of happiness through him—he, too, might soon know something of that glad music—and even the stately flight of the butterflies, which occasionally ventured over into the yard, stirred anticipations in him of joys to come.

The day waned slowly. The butterflies vanished; the rooks sailed homewards through the sunset; the wind dropped away, and the shadows of the high elms lengthened gradually and fell across the window.

The mysterious hour of the dusk, when the standard of reality changes and other worlds come close and listen, began to work its subtle spell upon his soul. Imperceptibly the shadows deepened as the veil of night drew silently across the sky. A gentle breathing filled the air; trees and fields were composing themselves to sleep; stars were peeping; wings were being folded.

But the boy's wings, trembling with life to the very tips of their long feathers, these were not being folded. Charged with excitement, like himself, they were gathering all their forces for the supreme effort of their first journey out into the open spaces where they might touch the secret sources of their own magical life.

For a long, long time he waited; but at last the trap-door lifted and Miss Lake appeared above the floor. The moment she stood in the room he noticed that her wings came through two little slits in her gown and folded down close to the body. They almost touched the ground.

"Hush!" she whispered, holding up a warning finger.

She came over on tiptoe and they began to talk in low whispers.

"He's on the watch; we must speak very quietly. We couldn't have a better night for it. The wind's in the south and the moon won't be up till we're well on our way."

Now that the actual moment was so near the boy felt something of fear steal over him. The night seemed so vast and terrible all of a sudden—like an immense black ocean with no friendly islands where they could fold their wings and rest.

"Don't waste your strength thinking," whispered the governess. "When the time comes, act quickly, that's all!"

She went over to the window and peered out cautiously, after a while beckoning the child to join her.

"He is there," she murmured in his ear. Jimbo could only make out an indistinct shadowy object crouching under the wall, and he was not even positive of that.

"Does he know we're going?" he asked in an awed whisper.

"He's there on the chance," she muttered, drawing back into the room. "When there's a possibility of any one getting frightened he's bound to be lurking about somewhere near. That's Fright all over. But he can't hurt you," she added, "because you're not going to get frightened. Besides, he can only fly when it's dark; and tonight we shall have the moon."

"I'm not afraid," declared the boy in spite of a rather fluttering heart.

"Are you ready?" was all she said.

At last, then, the moment had come. It was actually beside him, waiting, full of mystery and wonder, with alarm not far behind. The sun was buried below the horizon of the world, and the dusk had deepened into night. Stars were shining overhead; the leaves were motionless; not a breath stirred; the earth was silent and waiting.

"Yes, I'm ready," he whispered, almost inaudibly.

"Then listen," she said, "and I'll tell you exactly what to do: Jump upwards from the window ledge as high as you can, and the moment you begin to drop, open your wings and strike with all your might. You'll rise at once. The thing to remember is to *rise as quickly as possible*, because the wall prevents a long, easy, sweeping rise; and, whatever happens, you must clear that wall!"

"I shan't touch the ground then?" asked a faint little voice.

"Of course not! You'll get near it, but the moment you use your wings you'll stop sinking, and rise up, up, up, ever so quickly."

"And where to?"

"To me. You'll see me waiting for you above the trees. Steering will come naturally; it's quite easy."

Jimbo was already shaking with excitement. He could not help it. And he knew, in spite of all Miss Lake's care, that Fright was waiting in the yard to catch him if he fell, or sank too near the ground.

"I'll go first," added the governess, "and the moment you see that I've cleared the wall you must jump after me. Only do not keep me waiting!"

ALGERNON BLACKWOOD

The girl stood for a minute in silence, arranging her wings. Her fingers were trembling a little. Suddenly she drew the boy to her and kissed him passionately.

"Be brave!" she whispered, looking searchingly into his eyes, "and strike hard—you can't possibly fail."

In another minute she was climbing out of the window. For one second he saw her standing on the narrow ledge with black space at her feet; the next, without even a cry, she sprang out into the darkness, and was gone.

Jimbo caught his breath and ran up to see. She dropped like a stone, turning over sideways in the air, and then at once her wings opened on both sides and she righted. The darkness swallowed her up for a moment so that he could not see clearly, and only heard the threshing of the huge feathers; but it was easy to tell from the sound that she was rising.

Then suddenly a black form cleared the wall and rose swiftly in a magnificent sweep into the sky, and he saw her outlined darkly against the stars above the high elm tree. She was safe. Now it was his turn.

"Act quickly! Don't think!" rang in his ears. If only he could do it all as quickly as she had done it. But insidious fear had been working all the time below the surface, and his refusal to recognise it could not prevent it weakening his muscles and checking his power of decision. Fortunately something of his Older Self came to the rescue. The emotions of fear, excitement, and intense anticipation combined to call up the powers of his deeper being: the boy trembled horribly, but the old, experienced part of him sang with joy.

Cautiously he began to climb out on to the window-sill; first one foot and then the other hung over the edge. He sat there, staring down into black space beneath.

For a minute he hesitated; despair rushed over him in a wave; he could never take that awful jump into emptiness and darkness. It was impossible. Better be a prisoner for ever than risk so fearful a plunge. He felt cold, weak, frightened, and made a half-movement back into the room. The wings caught somehow between his legs and nearly flung him headlong into the yard.

"Jimbo! I'm waiting for you!" came at that moment in a faint cry from the stars, and the sound gave him just the impetus he needed before it was too late. He could not disappoint her—his faithful friend. Such a thing was impossible.

He stood upright on the ledge, his hands clutching the window-sash behind, balancing as best he could. He clenched his fists, drew a deep, long breath, and jumped upwards and forwards into the air.

Up rushed the darkness with a shriek; the air whistled in his ears; he dropped at fearful speed into nothingness.

At first everything was forgotten—wings, instructions, warnings, and all. He even forgot to open his wings at all, and in another second he would have been dashed upon the hard paving-stones of the courtyard where his great enemy lay waiting to seize him.

But just in the nick of time he remembered, and the long hours of practice bore fruit. Out flew the great red wings in a tremendous sweep on both sides of him, and he began to strike with every atom of strength he possessed. He had dropped to within six feet of the ground; but at once the strokes began to tell, and oh, magical sensation! he felt himself rising easily, lightly, swiftly.

A very slight effort of those big wings would have been sufficient to lift him out of danger, but in his terror and excitement he quite miscalculated their power, and in a single moment he was far out of reach of the dangerous yard and anything it contained. But the mad rush of it all made his head swim; he felt dizzy and confused, and, instead of clearing the wall, he landed on the top of it and clung to the crumbling coping with hands and feet, panting and breathless.

The dizziness was only momentary, however. In less than a minute he was on his feet and in the act of taking his second leap into space. This time it came more easily. He dropped, and the field swung up to meet him. Soon the powerful strokes of his wings drove him at great speed upwards, and he bounded ever higher towards the stars.

Overhead, the governess hovered like an immense bird, and as he rose up he caught the sound of her wings beating the air, while far beneath him, he heard with a shudder a voice like the rushing of a great river. It made him increase his pace, and in another minute he found himself among the little whirlwinds that raced about from the beating of Miss Lake's great wings.

"Well done!" cried the delighted governess. "Safe at last! Now we can fly to our heart's content!"

Jimbo flew up alongside, and together they dashed forward into the night.

XI

The First Flight

There was not much talking at first. The stress of conflicting emotions was so fierce that the words choked themselves in his throat, and the desire for utterance found its only vent in hard breathing.

The intoxication of rapid motion carried him away headlong in more senses than one. At first he felt as if he never would be able to keep up; then it seemed as if he never would get down again. For with wings it is almost easier to rise than to fall, and a first flight is, before anything else, a series of vivid and audacious surprises.

For a long time Jimbo was so dizzy with excitement and the novelty of the sensation that he forgot his deliverer altogether.

And what a flight it was! Instead of the steady race of the carrier pigeon, or of the rooks homeward bound at evening, it was the see-saw motion of the wren's swinging journey across the lawn; only heavier, faster, and with more terrific impetus. Up and down, each time with a rise and fall of twenty feet, he careered, whistling through the summer night; at the drop of each curve, so low that the scents of dewy grass rose into his face; at the crest of it, so high that the trees and hedges often became mere blots upon the dark surface of the earth.

The fields rushed by beneath him; the white roads flashed past like streaks of snow. Sometimes he shot across sheets of water and felt the cooler air strike his cheeks; sometimes over sheltered meadows, where the sunshine had slept all day and the air was still soft and warm; on and on, as easily as rain dropping from the sky, or wind rushing earthwards from between the clouds. Everything flew past him at an astonishing rate—everything but the bright stars that gazed calmly down overhead; and when he looked up and saw their steadfastness it helped to keep within bounds the fine alarm of this first excursion into the great vault of the sky.

"Gently, child!" gasped Miss Lake behind him. "We shall never keep it up at this rate."

"Oh! but it's so wonderful," he cried, drawing in the air loudly between his teeth, and shaking his wings rapidly like a hawk before it drops.

The pace slackened a little and the girl drew up alongside. For some time they flew forward together in silence.

They had been skirting the edge of a wood, when suddenly the trees fell away and Jimbo gave a scream and rose fifty feet into the air with a single bound. Straight in front of him loomed an immense, glaring disc that seemed to swim suddenly up into the sky above the trees. It hung there before his eyes and dazzled him.

"It's only the moon," cried Miss Lake from below.

Jimbo dropped through the air to her side again with a gasp.

"I thought it was a big hole in the sky with fire rushing through," he explained breathlessly.

The boy stared, full of wonder and delight, at the huge flaming circle that seemed to fill half the heavens in front of him.

"Look out!" cried the governess, seizing his hand.

Whish! whew! whirr! A large bird whipped past them like some winged imp of darkness, vanishing among the trees far below. There would certainly have been a collision but for the girl's energetic interference.

"You must be on the look-out for these night-birds," she said. "They fly so unexpectedly, and, of course, they don't see us properly. Telegraph wires and church steeples are bad too, but then we shan't fly over cities much. Keep a good height, it's safer."

They altered their course a little, flying at a different angle, so that the moon no longer dazzled them. Steering came quite easily by turning the body, and Jimbo still led the way, the governess following heavily and with a mighty business of wings and flapping.

It was something to remember, the glory of that first journey through the air. Sixty miles an hour, and scarcely an effort! Skimming the long ridges of the hills and rushing through the pure air of mountain tops; threading the star-beams; bathing themselves from head to foot in an ocean of cool, clean wind; swimming on the waves of viewless currents—currents warmed only by the magic of the stars, and kissed by the burning lips of flying meteors.

Far below them the moonlight touched the fields with silver and the murmur of the world rose faintly to their ears, trembling, as it were, with the inarticulate dreams of millions. Everywhere about them thrilled and sang the unspeakable power of the night. The mystery of its great heart seemed laid bare before them.

It was like a wonder-journey in some Eastern fairy tale. Sometimes they passed through zones of sweeter air, perfumed with the scents of

ALGERNON BLACKWOOD

hay and wild flowers; at others, the fresh, damp odour of ploughed fields rose up to them; or, again, they went spinning over leagues of forest where the tree-tops stretched beneath them like the surface of a wide, green sea, sleeping in the moonlight. And, when they crossed open water, the stars shone reflected in their faces; and all the while the wings, whirring and purring softly through the darkness, made pleasant music in their ears.

"I'm tired," declared Jimbo presently.

"Then we'll go down and rest," said his breathless companion with obvious relief.

She showed him how to spread his wings, sloping them towards the ground at an angle that enabled him to shoot rapidly downwards, at the same time regulating his speed by the least upward tilt. It was a glorious motion, without effort or difficulty, though the pace made it hard to keep the eyes open, and breathing became almost impossible. They dropped to within ten feet of the ground and then shot forward again.

But, while the boy was watching his companion's movements, and paying too little attention to his own, there rose suddenly before him out of the ground a huge, bulky form of something—and crash—he flew headlong into it.

Fortunately it was only a haystack; but the speed at which he was going lodged his head several inches under the thatch, whence he projected horizontally into space, feet, arms, and wings gyrating furiously. The governess, however, soon released him with much laughter, and they dropped down into the fallen hay upon the ground with no worse result than a shaking.

"Oh, what a lark!" he cried, shaking the hay out of his feathers, and rubbing his head rather ruefully.

"Except that larks are hardly night-birds," she laughed, helping him.

They settled with folded wings in the shadow of the haystack; and the big moon, peeping over the edge at them, must have surely wondered to see such a funny couple, in such a place, and at such an hour.

"Mushrooms!" suddenly cried the governess, springing to her feet. "There must be lots in this field. I'll go and pick some while you rest a bit."

Off she went, trapesing over the field in the moonlight, her wings folded behind her, her body bent a little forward as she searched, and in ten minutes she came back with her hands full. That was undoubtedly the time to enjoy mushrooms at their best, with the dew still on their tight little jackets, and the sweet odour of the earth caught under their umbrellas.

Soon they were all eaten, and Jimbo was lying back on a pile of hay, his shoulders against the wall of the stack, and his wings gathered round him like a warm cloak of feathers. He felt cosy and dozy, full of mushrooms inside and covered with hay and feathers outside. The governess had once told him that a sort of open-air sleep sometimes came after a long flight. It was, of course, not a real sleep, but a state in which everything about oneself is forgotten; no dreams, no movement, no falling asleep and waking up in the ordinary sense, but a condition of deep repose in which recuperation is very great.

Jimbo would have been greatly interested, no doubt, to know that his real body on the bed had also just been receiving nourishment, and was now passing into a quieter and less feverish condition. The parallel always held true between himself and his body in the nursery, but he could not know anything about this, and only supposed that it was this open-air sleep that he felt gently stealing over him.

It brought at first strange thoughts that carried him far away to other woods and other fields. While Miss Lake sat beside him eating her mushrooms, his mind was drawn off to some other little folk. But it was always stopped just short of them. He never could quite see their faces. Yet his thoughts continued their search, groping in the darkness; he felt sure he ought to be sharing his adventures with these other little persons, whoever they were; they ought to have been sitting beside him at that very moment, eating mushrooms, combing their wings, comparing the length of their feathers, and snuggling with him into the warm hay.

But they obstinately hovered just outside his memory, and refused to come in and surrender themselves. He could not remember who they were, and his yearnings went unsatisfied up to the stars, as yearnings generally do, while his thoughts returned weary from their search and he yielded to the seductions of the soothing open-air sleep.

The moon, meanwhile, rose higher and higher, drawing a silver veil over the stars. Upon the field the dews of midnight fell silently. A faint mist rose from the ground and covered the flowers in their dim seclusion under the hedgerows. The hours slipped away swiftly.

"Come on, Jimbo, boy!" cried the governess at length. "The moon's below the hills, and we must be off!"

The boy turned and stared sleepily at her from his nest in the hay.

"We've got miles to go. Remember the speed we came at!" she explained, getting up and arranging her wings.

Jimbo got up slowly and shook himself.

"I've been miles away," he said dreamily, "miles and miles. But I'm ready to start at once."

They looked about for a raised place to jump from. A ladder stood against the other side of the haystack. The governess climbed up it and Jimbo followed her drowsily. Hand in hand they sprang into the air from the edge of the thatched roof, and their wings spread out like sails to catch the wind. It smote their faces pleasantly as they plunged downwards and forwards, and the exhilarating rush of cool air banished from the boy's head the last vestige of the open-air sleep.

"We must keep up a good pace," cried the governess, taking a stream and the hedge beyond in a single sweep. "There's a light in the east already."

As she spoke a dog howled in a farmyard beneath them, and she shot upwards as though lifted by a sudden gust of wind.

"We're too low," she shouted from above. "That dog felt us near. Come up higher. It's easier flying, and we've got a long way to go."

Jimbo followed her up till they were several hundred feet above the earth and the keen air stung their cheeks. Then she led him still higher, till the meadows looked like the squares on a chess-board and the trees were like little toy shrubs. Here they rushed along at a tremendous speed, too fast to speak, their wings churning the air into little whirlwinds and eddies as they passed, whizzing, whistling, tearing through space.

The fields, however, were still dim in the shadows that precede the dawn, and the stars only just beginning to fade, when they saw the dark outline of the Empty House below them, and began carefully to descend. Soon they topped the high elms, startling the rooks into noisy cawing, and then, skimming the wall, sailed stealthily on outspread wings across the yard.

Cautiously dropping down to the level of the window, they crawled over the sill into the dark little room, and folded their wings.

XII

The Four Winds

The governess left the boy to his own reflections almost immediately. He spent the hours thinking and resting; going over again in his mind every incident of the great flight and wondering when the real, final escape would come, and what it would be like. Thus, between the two states of excitement he forgot for a while that he was still a prisoner, and the spell of horror was lifted temporarily from his heart.

The day passed quickly, and when Miss Lake appeared in the evening, she announced that there could be no flying again that night, and that she wished instead to give him important instruction for the future. There were rules, and signs, and times which he must learn carefully. The time might come when he would have to fly alone, and he must be prepared for everything.

"And the first thing I have to tell you," she said, exactly as though it was a schoolroom, "is: *Never fly over the sea.* Our kind of wings quickly absorb the finer particles of water and get clogged and heavy over the sea. You finally cannot resist the drawing power of the water, and you will be dragged down and drowned. So be very careful! When you are flying high it is often difficult to know where the land ends and the sea begins, especially on moonless nights. But you can always be certain of one thing: if there are no sounds below you—hoofs, voices, wheels, wind in trees—you are over the sea."

"Yes," said the child, listening with great attention. "And what else?"

"The next thing is: *Don't fly too high.* Though we fly like birds, remember we are not birds, and we can fly where they can't. We can fly in the ether—"

"Where's that?" he interrupted, half afraid of the sound.

She stooped and kissed him, laughing at his fear.

"There is nothing to be frightened about," she explained. "The air gets lighter and lighter as you go higher, till at last it stops altogether. Then there's only ether left. Birds can't fly in ether because it's too thin. We can, because—"

"Is that why it was good for me to get lighter and thinner?" he interrupted again in a puzzled voice.

"Partly, yes."

"And what happens in the ether, please?" It still frightened him a little.

"Nothing—except that if you fly too high you reach a point where the earth ceases to hold you, and you dash off into space. Weight leaves you then, and the wings move without effort. Faster and faster you rush upwards, till you lose all control of your movements, and then—"

Miss Lake hesitated a moment.

"And then—?" asked the fascinated child.

"You may never come down again," she said slowly. "You may be sucked into anything that happens to come your way—a comet, or a shooting star, or the moon."

"I should like a shooting star best," observed the boy, deeply interested. "The moon frightens me, I think. It looks so dreadfully clean."

"You won't like any of them when the time comes," she laughed. "No one ever gets out again who once gets in. But you'll never be caught that way after what I've told you," she added, with decision.

"I shall never want to fly as high as that, I'm sure," said Jimbo. "And now, please, what comes next?"

The next thing, she went on to explain, was the *weather*, which, to all flying creatures, was of the utmost importance. Before starting for a flight he must always carefully consider the state of the sky, and the direction in which he wished to go. For this purpose he must master the meaning and character of the Four Winds and be able to recognise them in a moment.

"Once you know these," she said, "you cannot possibly go wrong. To make it easier, I've put each Wind into a little simple rhyme, for you."

"I'm listening," he said eagerly.

"The North Wind is one of the worst and most dangerous, because it blows so much faster than you think. It's taken you ten miles before you think you've gone two. In starting with a North Wind, always fly *against* it; then it will bring you home easily. If you fly *with* it, you may be swept so far that the day will catch you before you can get home; and then you're as good as lost. Even birds fly warily when this wind is about. It has no lulls or resting-places in it; it blows steadily on and on, and conquers everything it comes against—everything except the mountains."

"And its rhyme?" asked Jimbo, all ears.

> *"It will show you the joy of the birds, my child,*
> *You shall know their terrible bliss;*
> *It will teach you to hide, when the night is wild,*
> *From the storm's too passionate kiss.*
> *For the Wind of the North*
> *Is a volleying forth*
> *That will lift you with springs*
> *In the heart of your wings,*
> *And may sweep you away*
> *To the edge of the day.*
> *So, beware of the Wind of the North, my child,*
> *Fly not with the Wind of the North!"*

"I think I like him all the same," said Jimbo. "But I'll remember always to fly against him."

"The East Wind is worse still, for it hurts," continued the governess. "It stings and cuts. It's like the breath of an ice-creature; it brings hail and sleet and cold rain that beat down wings and blind the eyes. Like the North Wind, too, it is dreadfully swift and full of little whirlwinds, and may easily carry you into the light of day that would prove your destruction. Avoid it always; no hiding-place is safe from it. This is the rhyme:

> *"It will teach you the secrets the eagles know*
> *Of the tempests' and whirlwinds' birth;*
> *And the magical weaving of rain and snow*
> *As they fall from the sky to the earth.*
> *But an Easterly wind*
> *Is for ever unkind;*
> *It will torture and twist you*
> *And never assist you,*
> *But will drive you with might*
> *To the verge of the night.*
> *So, beware of the Wind of the East, my child,*
> *Fly not with the Wind of the East."*

"The West Wind is really a very nice and jolly wind in itself," she went on, "but it's dangerous for a special reason: *it will carry you out to sea.* The Empty House is only a few miles from the coast, and a strong West

Wind would take you there almost before you had time to get down to earth again. And there's no use struggling against a really steady West Wind, for it's simply tireless. Luckily, it rarely blows at night, but goes down with the sun. Often, too, it blows hard to the coast, and then drops suddenly, leaving you among the fogs and mists of the sea."

"Rather a nice, exciting sort of wind though," remarked Jimbo, waiting for the rhyme.

> *"So, at last, you shall know from their lightest breath*
> *To which heaven each wind belongs;*
> *And shall master their meaning for life or death*
> *By the shout of their splendid songs.*
> *Yet the Wind of the West*
> *Is a wind unblest;*
> *It is lifted and kissed*
> *By the spirits of mist;*
> *It will clasp you and flee*
> *To the wastes of the sea.*
> *So, beware of the Wind of the West, my child,*
> *Fly not with the Wind of the West!"*

"A jolly wind," observed Jimbo again. "But that doesn't leave much over to fly with," he added sadly. "They all seem dangerous or cruel."

"Yes," she laughed, "and so they are till you can master them—then they're kind, only one that's really always safe and kind is the Wind of the South. It's a sweet, gentle wind, beloved of all that flies, and you can't possibly mistake it. You can tell it at once by the murmuring way it stirs the grasses and the tops of the trees. Its taste is soft and sweet in the mouth like wine, and there's always a faint perfume about it like gardens in summer. It is the joy of this wind that makes all flying things sing. With a South Wind you can go anywhere and no harm can come to you."

"Dear old South Wind," cried Jimbo, rubbing his hands with delight. "I hope it will blow soon."

"Its rhyme is very easy, too, though you will always be able to tell it without that," she added.

> *"For this is the favourite Wind of all,*
> *Beloved of the stars and night;*
> *In the rustle of leaves you shall hear it call*

> *To the passionate joys of flight.*
> *It will carry you forth in its wonderful hair*
> *To the far-away courts of the sky,*
> *And the breath of its lips is a murmuring prayer*
> *For the safety of all who fly.*
> *For the Wind of the South*
> *Is like wine in the mouth,*
> *With its whispering showers*
> *And perfume of flowers,*
> *When it falls like a sigh*
> *From the heart of the sky."*

"Oh!" interrupted Jimbo, rubbing his hands, "that *is* nice. That's *my* wind!"

> *"It will bear you aloft*
> *With a pressure so soft*
> *That you hardly shall guess*
> *Whose the gentle caress."*

"Hooray!" he cried again.

> *"It's the kindest of weathers*
> *For our red feathers,*
> *And blows open the way*
> *To the Gardens of Play.*
> *So, fly out with the Wind of the South, my child,*
> *With the wonderful Wind of the South."*

"Oh, I love the South Wind already," he shouted, clapping his hands again. "I hope it will blow very, *very* soon."

"It may be rising even now," answered the governess, leading him to the window. But, as they gazed at the summer landscape lying in the fading light of the sunset, all was still and resting. The air was hushed, the leaves motionless. There was no call just then to flight from among the tree-tops, and he went back into the room disappointed.

"But why can't we escape at once?" he asked again, after he had given his promise to remember all she had told him, and to be extra careful if he ever went out flying alone.

ALGERNON BLACKWOOD

"Jimbo, dear, I've told you before, it's because your body isn't ready for you yet," she answered patiently. "There's hardly any circulation in it, and if you forced your way back now the shock might stop your heart beating altogether. Then you'd be really dead, and escape would be impossible."

The boy sat on the edge of the bed staring intently at her while she spoke. Something clutched at his heart. He felt his Older Self, with its greater knowledge, rising up out of the depths within him. The child struggled with the old soul for possession.

"Have *you* got any circulation?" he asked abruptly at length. "I mean, has *your* heart stopped beating?"

But the smile called up by his words froze on her lips. She crossed to the window and stood with her back to the fading light, avoiding his eyes.

"My case, Jimbo, is a little different from yours," she said presently. "The important thing is to make certain about your escape. Never mind about me."

"But escape without you is nothing," he said, the Older Self now wholly in possession. "I simply wouldn't go. I'd rather stay here—with you."

The governess made no reply, but she turned her back to the room and leaned out of the window. Jimbo fancied he heard a sob. He felt a great big heart swelling up within his little body, and he crossed over beside her. For some minutes they stood there in silence, watching the stars that were already shining faintly in the sky.

"Whatever happens," he said, nestling against her, "I shan't go from here without you. Remember that!"

He was going to say a lot more, but somehow or other, when she stooped over to kiss his head—he hardly came up to her shoulder—it all ran suddenly out of his mind, and the little child dropped back into possession again. The tide of his thoughts that seemed about to rise, fast and furious, sank away completely, leaving his mind a clean-washed slate without a single image; and presently, without any more words, the governess left him and went through the trap-door into the silence and mystery of the house below.

Several hours later, about the middle of the night, there came over him a most disagreeable sensation of nausea and dizziness. The ground rose and fell beneath his feet, the walls swam about sideways, and the ceiling slid off into the air. It only lasted a few minutes, however, and

Jimbo knew from what she had told him that it was the Flying Sickness which always followed the first long flight.

But, about the same time, another little body, lying in a night-nursery bed, was being convulsed with a similar attack; and the sickness of the little prisoner in the Empty House had its parallel, strangely enough, in the half-tenanted body miles away in a different world.

XIII

PLEASURES OF FLIGHT

Since the night when Jimbo had nearly fallen into the yard and risked capture, Fright, the horrible owner of the house, had kept himself well out of the way, and had allowed himself to be neither seen nor heard.

But the boy was not foolish enough to fall into the other trap, and imagine, therefore, that He did not know what was going on. Jimbo felt quite sure that He was only waiting his chance; and the governess's avoidance of the subject tended to confirm this supposition.

"He's disappeared somewhere and taken the children with him," she declared when he questioned her. "And now you know almost as much as I do."

"But not quite!" he laughed mischievously.

"Enough, though," she replied. "We want all our energy for escape when it comes. Don't bother about anything else for the moment."

During the day, when he was alone, his thoughts and fancies often terrified him; but at night, when he was rushing through the heavens, the intense delight of flying drove all minor emotions out of his consciousness, and he even forgot his one great desire—to escape. One night, however, something happened that brought it back more keenly than ever.

He had been out flying alone, but had not gone far when he noticed that an easterly wind had begun to rise and was blowing steadily behind him. With the recent instructions fresh in his head, he thought it wiser to turn homewards rather than fight his way back later against a really strong wind from this quarter. Flying low along the surface of the fields so as to avoid its full force, he suddenly rose up with a good sweep and settled on the top of the wall enclosing the yard.

The moonlight lay bright over everything. His approach had been very quiet. He was just about to sail across to the window when something caught his eye, and he hesitated a moment, and stared.

Something was moving at the other end of the courtyard.

It seemed to him that the moonlight suddenly grew pale and ghastly; the night air turned chilly; shivers began to run up and down his back.

He folded his wings and watched.

At the end of the yard he saw several figures moving busily to and fro in the shadow of the wall. They were very small; but close beside them all the time stood a much larger figure which seemed to be directing their movements. There was no need to look twice; it was impossible to mistake these terrible little people and their hideous overseer. Horror rushed over the boy, and a wild scream was out in the night before he could possibly prevent it. At the same moment a cloud passed over the face of the moon and the yard was shrouded in darkness.

A minute later the cloud passed off; but while it was still too dark to see clearly, Jimbo was conscious of a rushing, whispering sound in the air, and something went past him at a tremendous pace into the sky. The wind stirred his hair as it passed, and a moment later he heard voices far away in the distance—up in the sky or within the house he could not tell—singing mournfully the song he now knew so well:—

We dance with phantoms and with shadows play.

But when he looked down at the yard he saw that it was deserted, and the corner by the little upright stones lay in the clear moonlight, empty of figures, large or small.

Shivering with fright, he flew across to the window ledge, and almost tumbled into the arms of the governess who was standing close inside.

"What's the matter, child?" she asked in a voice that trembled a little.

And, still shuddering, he told her how he thought he had seen the children working by the gravestones. All her efforts to calm him at first failed, but after a bit she drew his thoughts to pleasanter things, and he was not so certain after all that he had not been deceived by the cunning of the moonlight and the shadows.

A long interval passed, and no further sign was given by the owner of the house or his band of frightened children. Jimbo soon lost himself again in the delights of flying and the joy of his increasing powers.

Most of all he enjoyed the quiet, starlit nights before the moon was up; for the moon dazzled the eyes in the rarefied air where they flew, whereas the stars gave just enough light to steer by without making it uncomfortable.

Moreover, the moon often filled him with a kind of faint terror, as of death; he could never gaze at her white face for long without feeling that something entered his heart with those silver rays—something that boded him no good. He never spoke of this to the governess; indeed, he only recognised it himself when the moon was near the full; but it lay always in the depths of his being, and he felt dimly that it would have to be reckoned with before he could really escape for good. He took no liberties when the moon was at the full.

He loved to hover—for he had learned by this time that most difficult of all flying feats; to hold the body vertical and whirr the wings without rising or advancing—he loved to hover on windless nights over ponds and rivers and see the stars reflected in their still pools. Indeed, sometimes he hovered till he dropped, and only saved himself from a wetting by sweeping up in a tremendous curve along the surface of the water, and thus up into the branches of the trees where the governess sat waiting for him. And then, after a little rest, they would launch forth again and fly over fields and woods, sometimes even as far as the hills that ran down the coast of the sea itself.

They usually flew at a height of about a thousand feet, and the earth passed beneath them like a great streaked shadow. But as soon as the moon was up the whole country turned into a fairyland of wonder. Her light touched the woods with a softened magic, and the fields and hedges became frosted most delicately. Beneath a thin transparency of mist the water shone with a silvery brilliance that always enabled them to distinguish it from the land at any height; while the farms and country houses were swathed in tender grey shadows through which the trees and chimneys pierced in slender lines of black. It was wonderful to watch the shadows everywhere spinning their blue veil of distance that lent even to the commonest objects something of enchantment and mystery.

Those were wonderful journeys they made together into the pathways of the silent night, along the unknown courses, into that hushed centre where they could almost hear the beatings of her great heart—like winged thoughts searching the huge vault, till the boy ached with the sensations of speed and distance, and the old yellow moon seemed to stagger across the sky.

Sometimes they rose very high into freezing air, so high that the earth became a dull shadow specked with light. They saw the trains running in all directions with thin threads of smoke shining in the glare of the open fire-boxes. But they seemed very tiny trains indeed, and stirred in him no recollections of the semi-annual visits to London town when he went to the dentist, and lunched with the dreaded grandmother or the stiff and fashionable aunts.

And when they came down again from these perilous heights, the scents of the earth rose to meet them, the perfume of woods and fields, and the smells of the open country.

There was, too, the delight, the curious delight of windy nights, when the wind smote and buffeted them, knocking them suddenly sideways, whistling through their feathers as if it wanted to tear them from their sockets; rushing furiously up underneath their wings with repeated blows; turning them round, and backwards and forwards, washing them from head to foot in a tempestuous sea of rapid and unexpected motion.

It was, of course, far easier to fly with a wind than without one. The difficulty with a violent wind was to get down—not to keep up. The gusts drove up against the under-surfaces of their wings and kept them afloat, so that by merely spreading them like sails they could sweep and circle without a single stroke. Jimbo soon learned to manoeuvre so that he could turn the strength of a great wind to his own purposes, and revel in its boisterous waves and currents like a strong swimmer in a rough sea.

And to listen to the wind as it swept backwards and forwards over the surface of the earth below was another pleasure; for everything it touched gave out a definite note. He soon got to know the long sad cry from the willows, and the little whispering in the tops of the poplar trees; the crisp, silvery rattle of the birches, and the deep roar from oaks and beech woods. The sound of a forest was like the shouting of the sea.

But far more lovely, when they descended a little, and the wind was more gentle, were the low pipings among the reeds and the little wayward murmurs under the hedgerows.

The pine trees, however, drew them most, with their weird voices, now far away, now near, rising upwards with a wind of sighs.

There was a grove of these trees that trooped down to the waters of a little lake in the hills, and to this spot they often flew when the wind was low and the music likely, therefore, to be to their taste. For, even when there was no perceptible wind, these trees seemed always full of mysterious, mournful whisperings; their branches held soft music that never quite died away, even when all other trees were silent and motionless.

Besides these special expeditions, they flew everywhere and anywhere.

ALGERNON BLACKWOOD

They visited the birds in their nests in lofty trees, and exchanged the time of night with wise-eyed owls staring out upon them from the ivy. They hovered up the face of great cliffs, and passed the hawks asleep on perilous ledges; skimmed over lonely marshes, frightening the water-birds paddling in and out among the reeds. They followed the windings of streams, singing among the meadows, and flew along the wet sands as they watched the moon rise out of the sea.

These flights were unadulterated pleasure, and Jimbo thought he could never have enough of them.

He soon began to notice, too, that the trees emanated something that affected his own condition. When he sat in their branches this was very noticeable. Currents of force passed from them into himself. And even when he flew over their crests he was aware that some woods exhaled vigorous, life-giving forces, while others tired and depleted him. Nothing was visible actually, but fine waves seemed to beat up against his eyes and thoughts, making him stronger or weaker, happy or melancholy, full of hope and courage, or listless and indifferent.

These emanations of the trees—this giving-forth of their own personal forces—were, of course, very varied in strength and character. Oaks and pines were the best combination, he found, before the stress of a long flight, the former giving him steadiness, and the latter steely endurance and the power to steer in sinuous, swift curves, without taking thought or trouble.

Other trees gave other powers. All gave something. It was impossible to sit among their branches without absorbing some of the subtle and exhilarating tree-life. He soon learned how to gather it all into himself, and turn it to account in his own being.

"Sit quietly," the governess said. "Let the forces creep in and stir about. Do nothing yourself. Give them time to become part of yourself and mix properly with your own currents. Effort on your part prevents this, and you weaken them without gaining anything yourself."

Jimbo made all sorts of experiments with trees and rocks and water and fields, learning gradually the different qualities of force they gave forth, and how to use them for himself. Nothing, he found, was really dead. And sometimes he got himself into strange difficulties in the beginning of his attempts to master and absorb these nature-forces.

"Remember," the governess warned him more than once, when he was inclined to play tricks, "they are in quite a different world to ours. You cannot take liberties with them. Even a sympathetic soul like yourself only touches the fringe of their world. You exchange surface-messages with them, nothing more. Some trees have terrible forces just below the surface. They could extinguish you altogether—absorb you into themselves. Others are naturally hostile. Some are mere tricksters. Others are shifty and treacherous, like the hollies, that move about too much. The oak and the pine and the elm are friendly, and you can always trust them absolutely. But there are others—!"

She held up a warning finger, and Jimbo's eyes nearly dropped out of his head.

"No," she added, in reply to his questions, "you can't learn all this at once. Perhaps—" She hesitated a little. "Perhaps, if you don't escape, we should have time for all manner of adventures among the trees and other things—but then, we *are* going to escape, so there's no good wasting time over *that*!"

XIV

An Adventure

B ut Miss Lake did not always accompany him on these excursions into the night; sometimes he took long flights by himself, and she rather encouraged him in this, saying it would give him confidence in case he ever lost her and was obliged to find his way about alone.

"But I couldn't get really lost," he said once to her. "I know the winds perfectly now and the country round for miles, and I never go out in fog—"

"But these are only practice flights," she replied. "The flight of escape is a very different matter. I want you to learn all you possibly can so as to be prepared for anything."

Jimbo felt vaguely uncomfortable when she talked like this.

"But you'll be with me in the Escape Flight—the final one of all," he said; "and nothing ever goes wrong when you're with me."

"I should like to be always with you," she answered tenderly, "but it's well to be prepared for anything, just the same."

And more than this the boy could never get out of her.

On one of these lonely flights, however, he made the unpleasant discovery that he was being followed.

At first he only imagined there was somebody after him because of the curious vibrations of the very rarefied air in which he flew. Every time his flight slackened and the noise of his own wings grew less, there reached him from some other corner of the sky a sound like the vibrations of large wings beating the air. It seemed behind, and generally below him, but the swishing of his own feathers made it difficult to hear with distinctness, or to be certain of the direction.

Evidently it was a long way off; but now and again, when he took a spurt and then sailed silently for several minutes on outstretched wings, the beating of distant, following feathers seemed unmistakably clear, and he raced on again at full speed more than terrified. Other times, however, when he tried to listen, there was no trace of this other flyer, and then his fear would disappear, and he would persuade himself that it had been imagination. So much on these flights he knew to be imagination—the sentences, voices, and laughter, for instance, that filled the air and sounded so real, yet were actually caused by the wind rushing past his ears, the rhythm of the wing-beats, and the tips of the feathers occasionally rubbing against the sides of his body.

But at last one night the suspicion that he was followed became a certainty.

He was flying far up in the sky, passing over some big city, when the sound rose to his ears, and he paused, sailing on stretched wings, to listen. Looking down into the immense space below, he saw, plainly outlined against the luminous patch above the city, the form of a large flying creature moving by with rapid strokes. The pulsations of its great wings made the air tremble so that he both heard and felt them. It may have been that the vapours of the city distorted the thing, just as the earth's atmosphere magnifies the rising or setting of the moon; but, even so, it was easy to see that it was something a good deal larger than himself, and with a much more powerful flight.

Fortunately, it did not seem this time to be actually on his trail, for it swept by at a great pace, and was soon lost in the darkness far ahead. Perhaps it was only searching for him, and his great height had proved his safety. But in any case he was exceedingly terrified, and at once turned round, pointed his head for the earth, and shot downwards in the direction of the Empty House as fast as ever he could.

But when he spoke to the governess she made light of it, and told him there was nothing to be afraid of. It might have been a flock of hurrying night-birds, she said, or an owl distorted by the city's light, or even his own reflection magnified in water. Anyhow, she felt sure it was not chasing him, and he need pay no attention to it.

Jimbo felt reassured, but not quite satisfied. He knew a flying monster when he saw one; and it was only when he had been for many more flights alone, without its reappearance, that his confidence was fully restored, and he began to forget about it.

Certainly these lonely flights were very much to his taste. His Older Self, with its dim hauntings of a great memory somewhere behind him, took possession then, and he was able to commune with nature in a way that the presence of the governess made impossible. With her his Older Self rarely showed itself above the surface for long; he was always the child. But, when alone, Nature became alive; he drew force from the trees and flowers, and felt that they all shared a common life together. Had he been imprisoned by some wizard of old in a tree-form, knowing of the sunset and the dawn only by the sweet messages that

ALGERNON BLACKWOOD

rustled in his branches, the wind could hardly have spoken to him with a more intimate meaning; or the life of the fields, eternally patient, have touched him more nearly with their joys and sorrows. It seemed almost as if, from his leafy cell, he had gazed before this into the shining pools with which the summer rains jewelled the meadows, sending his soul in a stream of unsatisfied yearning up to the stars. It all came back dimly when he heard the wind among the leaves, and carried him off to the woods and fields of an existence far antedating this one—

And on gentle nights, when the wind itself was half asleep and dreaming, the pine trees drew him most of all, for theirs was the song he loved above all others. He would fly round and round the little grove by the mountain lake, listening for hours together to their sighing voices. But the governess was never told of this, whatever she may have guessed; for it seemed to him a joy too deep for words, the pains and sweetness being mingled too mysteriously for him ever to express in awkward sentences. Moreover, it all passed away and was forgotten the moment the child took possession and usurped the older memory.

One night, when the moon was high and the air was cool and fragrant after the heat of the day, Jimbo felt a strong desire to get off by himself for a long flight. He was full of energy, and the space-craving cried to be satisfied. For several days he had been content with slow, stupid expeditions with the governess.

"I'm off alone tonight," he cried, balancing on the window ledge, "but I'll be back before dawn. Good-bye!"

She kissed him, as she always did now, and with her good-bye ringing in his ears, he dropped from the window and rose rapidly over the elms and away from earth.

This night, for some reason, the stars and the moon seemed to draw him, and with tireless wings he mounted up, up, up, to a height he had never reached before. The intoxication of the strong night air rose into his brain and he dashed forward ever faster, with a mad delight, into the endless space before him.

Mile upon mile lay behind him as he rushed onwards, always pointing a little on the upward slope, drunk with speed. The earth faded away to a dark expanse of shadow beneath him, and he no longer was conscious of the deep murmur that usually flowed steadily upwards from its surface. He had often before risen out of reach of the earth noises, but never so far that this dull reverberating sound, combined of all the voices of the world merged together, failed to make itself heard.

Tonight, however, he heard nothing. The stars above his head changed from yellow to diamond white, and the cold air stung his cheeks and brought the water to his eyes.

But at length the governess's warning, as he explored these forbidden regions, came back to him, and in a series of gigantic bounds that took his breath away completely, he dropped nearer to the earth again and kept on at a much lower level.

The hours passed and the position of the moon began to alter noticeably. Some of the constellations that were overhead when he started were now dipping below the horizon. Never before had he ventured so far from home, and he began to realise that he had been flying much longer than he knew or intended. The speed had been terrific.

The change came imperceptibly. With the discovery that his wings were not moving quite so easily as before, he became suddenly aware that this had really been the case for some little time. He was flying with greater effort, and for a long time this effort had been increasing gradually before he actually recognised the fact.

Although no longer pointing towards the earth he seemed to be sinking. It became increasingly difficult to fly upwards. His wings did not seem to fail or weaken, nor was he conscious of feeling tired; but something was ever persuading him to fly lower, almost as if a million tiny threads were coaxing him downwards, drawing him gradually nearer to the world again. Whatever it was, the earth had come much closer to him in the last hour, and its familiar voices were pleasant to hear after the boundless heights he had just left.

But for some reason his speed grew insensibly less and less. His wings moved apparently as fast as before, but it was harder to keep up. In spite of himself he kept sinking. The sensation was quite new, and he could not understand it. It almost seemed as though he were being *pulled* downwards.

Jimbo began to feel uneasy. He had not lost his bearings, but he was a very long way from home, and quite beyond reach of the help he was so accustomed to. With a great effort he mounted several hundred feet into the air, and tried hard to stay there. For a short time he succeeded, but he soon felt himself sinking gradually downwards again. The force drawing him was a constant force without rise or fall; and with a deadly feeling of fear the boy began to realise that he would soon have to yield to it altogether. His heart beat faster and his thoughts turned to the friend who was then far away, but who alone could save him.

　　　　　　　　　　　　　　　　　　　ALGERNON BLACKWOOD

She, at least, could have explained it and told him what best to do. But the governess was beyond his reach. This problem he must face alone.

Something, however, had to be done quickly, and Jimbo, acting more as the man than as the boy, turned and flew hurriedly forward in another direction. He hoped this might somehow counteract the force that still drew him downwards; and for a time it apparently did so, and he flew level. But the strain increased every minute, and he looked down with something of a shudder as he realised that before very long he would be obliged to yield to this deadly force—and drop!

It was then for the first time he noticed a change had come over the surface of the earth below. Instead of the patchwork of field and wood and road, he saw a vast cloud stretching out, white and smooth in the moonlight. The world was hidden beneath a snowy fog, dense and impenetrable. It was no longer even possible to tell in what direction he was flying, for there was nothing to steer by. This was a new and unexpected complication, and the boy could not understand how the change had come about so quickly; the last time he had glanced down for indications to steer by, everything had been clear and easily visible.

It was very beautiful, this carpet of white mist with the silver moon shining upon it, but it thrilled him now with an unpleasant sense of dread. And, still more unpleasant, was a new sound which suddenly broke in upon the stillness and turned his blood into ice. He was certain that he heard wings behind him. He was being followed, and this meant that it was impossible to turn and fly back.

There was nothing now to do but fly forwards and hope to distance the huge wings; but if he was being followed by the powerful flyer he had seen a few nights before, the boy knew that he stood little chance of success, and he only did it because it seemed the one thing possible.

The cloud was dense and chill as he entered it; its moisture clung to his wings and made them heavy; his muscles seemed to stiffen, and motion became more and more difficult. The wings behind him meanwhile came closer.

He was flying along the surface of the mist now, his body and wings hidden, and his head just above the level. He could see along its white, even top. If he sank a few more inches it would be impossible to see at all, or even to judge where he was going. Soon it rose level with his lips, and at the same time he noticed a new smell in the air, faint at first, but growing every moment stronger. It was a fresh, sweet odour, yet it somehow added to his alarm, and stirred in him new centres of uneasiness. He tried vainly to increase his speed and distance the wings which continued to gain so steadily upon him from behind.

The cloud, apparently, was not everywhere of the same density, for here and there he saw the tops of green hills below him as he flew. But he could not understand why each green hill seemed to have a little lake on its summit—a little lake in which the reflected moon stared straight up into his face. Nor could he quite make out what the sounds were which rose to his ears through the muffling of the cloud—sounds of tumultuous rushing, hissing, and tumbling. They were continuous, these sounds, and once or twice he thought he heard with them a deep, thunderous roar that almost made his heart stop beating as he listened.

Was he, perhaps, over a range of high mountains, and was this the sound of the tumbling torrents?

Then, suddenly, it came to him with a shock that the ordinary sounds of the earth had wholly ceased.

Jimbo felt his head beginning to whirl. He grew weaker every minute; less able to offer resistance to the remorseless forces that were sucking him down. Now the mist had closed over his head, and he could no longer see the moonlight. He turned again, shaking with terror, and drove forward headlong through the clinging vapour. A sensation of choking rose in his throat; he was tired out, ready to drop with exhaustion. The wings of the following creature were now so close that he thought every minute he would be seized from behind and plunged into the abyss to his death.

It was just then that he made the awful discovery that the world below him was not stationary: the *green hills were moving*. They were sweeping past with a rushing, thundering sound in regular procession; and their huge sides were streaked with white. The reflection of the moon leaped up into his face as each hill rolled hissing and gurgling by, and he knew at last with a shock of unutterable horror that it was The Sea!

He was flying over the sea, and the waters were drawing him down. The immense, green waves that rolled along through the sea fog, carrying the moon's face on their crests, foaming and gurgling as they went, were already leaping up to seize him by the feet and drag him into their depths.

He dropped several feet deeper into the mist, and towards the sea, terror-stricken and blinded. Then, turning frantically, not knowing what else to do, he struck out, with his last strength, for the upper surface and the moonlight. But as he did so, turning his face towards the sky he saw a dark form hovering just above him, covering his retreat with huge outstretched wings. It was too late; he was hemmed in on all sides.

At that moment a huge, rolling wave, bigger than all the rest, swept past and wet him to the knees. His heart failed him. The next wave would cover him. Already it was rushing towards him with foaming crest. He was in its shadow; he heard its thunder. Darkness rushed over him—he saw the vast sides streaked with grey and white—when suddenly, the owner of the wings plucked him in the back, mid-way between the shoulders, and lifted him bodily out of the fog, so that the wave swept by without even wetting his feet.

The next minute he saw a dim, white sheet of silvery mist at his feet, and found himself far above it in the sweet, clean moonlight; and when he turned, almost dead with terror, to look upon his captor, he found himself looking straight into the eyes of—the governess.

The sense of relief was so great that Jimbo simply closed his wings, and hung, a dead weight, in the air.

"Use your wings!" cried the governess sharply; and, still holding him, while he began to flap feebly, she turned and flew in the direction of the land.

"You!" he gasped at last. "It was you following me!"

"Of course it was me! I never let you out of my sight. I've always followed you—every time you've been out alone."

Jimbo was still conscious of the drawing power of the sea, but he felt that his companion was too strong for it. After fifteen minutes of fierce flight he heard the sounds of earth again, and knew that they were safe.

Then the governess loosened her hold, and they flew along side by side in the direction of home.

"I won't scold you, Jimbo," she said presently, "for you've suffered enough already." She was the first to break the silence, and her voice trembled a little. "But remember, the sea draws you down, just as surely as the moon draws you up. Nothing would please Him better than to see you destroyed by one or the other."

Jimbo said nothing. But, when once they were safe inside the room again, he went up and cried his eyes out on her arm, while she folded him in to her heart as if he were the only thing in the whole world she had to love.

XV

The Call of the Body

One night, towards the end of the practice flights, a strange thing happened, which showed that the time for the final flight of escape was drawing near.

They had been out for several hours flying through a rainstorm, the thousand little drops of which stung their faces like tiny gun-shot. About two in the morning the wind shifted and drove the clouds away as by magic; the stars came out, at first like the eyes of children still dim with crying, but later with a clear brilliance that filled Jimbo and the governess with keen pleasure. The air was washed and perfumed; the night luminous, alive, singing. All its tenderness and passion entered their hearts and filled them with the wonder of its glory.

"Come down, Jimbo," said the governess, "and we'll lie in the trees and smell the air after the rain."

"Yes," added the boy, whose Older Self had been whispering mysterious things to him, "and watch the stars and hear them singing."

He led the way to some beech trees that lined a secluded lane, and settled himself comfortably in the top branches of the largest, while the governess soon found a resting-place beside him. It was a deserted spot, far from human habitation. Here and there through the foliage they could see little pools of rain-water reflecting the sky. The group of trees swung in the wind, dreaming great woodland dreams, and overhead the stars looked like a thousand orchards in the sky, filling the air with the radiance of their blossoms.

"How brilliant they are tonight," said the governess, after watching the boy attentively for some minutes as they lay side by side in the great forked branch. "I never saw the constellations so clear."

"But they have so little shape," he answered dreamily; "if we wore lights when we flew about we should make much better constellations than they do."

"The Big and Little Child instead of the Big and Little Bear," she laughed, still watching him.

"I'm slipping away—" he began, and then stopped suddenly. He saw the expression of his companion's eyes, which were looking him through and through with the most poignant love and yearning mingled in their gaze, and something clutched at his heart that he could not understand.

"—not slipping out of the tree," he went on vaguely, "but slipping into some new place or condition. I don't understand it. Am I—going off somewhere—where you can't follow? I thought suddenly—I was losing you."

The governess smiled at him sadly and said nothing. She stroked his wings and then raised them to her lips and kissed them. Jimbo watched her, and folded his other wing across into her hands; he felt unhappy, and his heart began to swell within him; but he didn't know what to say, and the Older Self began slowly to fade away again.

"But the stars," he went on, "have they got things they send out too—forces, I mean, like the trees? Do they send out something that makes us feel sad, or happy, or strong, or weak?"

She did not answer for some time; she lay watching his face and fondling his smooth red wings; and, presently, when she did begin to explain, Jimbo found that the child in him was then paramount again, and he could not quite follow what she said.

He tried to answer properly and seem interested, but her words were very long and hard to understand, and after a time he thought she was talking to herself more than to him, and he gave up all serious effort to follow. Then he became aware that her voice had changed. The words seemed to drop down upon him from a great height. He imagined she was standing on one of those far stars he had been asking about, and was shouting at him through an immense tube of sky and darkness. The words pricked his ears like needle-points, only he no longer heard them as words, but as tiny explosions of sound, meaningless and distant. Swift flashes of light began to dance before his eyes, and suddenly from underneath the tree, a wind rose up and rushed, laughing, across his face. Darkness in a mass dropped over his eyes, and he sank backwards somewhere into another corner of space altogether.

The governess, meanwhile, lay quite still, watching the limp form in the branches beside her and still holding the tips of his red wings. Presently tears stole into her eyes, and began to run down her cheeks. One deep sigh after another escaped from her lips; but the little boy, or the old soul, who was the cause of all her emotion, apparently was far away and knew nothing of it. For a long time she lay in silence, and then leaned a little nearer to him, so as to see his full face. The eyes were wide open and staring, but they were looking at nothing she could see, for the consciousness cannot be in two places at the same time, and Jimbo just then was off on a little journey of his own, a journey that was but preliminary to the great final one of all.

"Jimbo," whispered the girl between her tears and sighs, "Jimbo! Where have you gone to? Tell me, are they getting ready for you at last, and am I to lose you after all? Is this the only way I can save you—by losing you?"

There was no answer, no sign of movement; and the governess hid her face in her hands and cried quietly to herself, while her tears dropped down through the branches of the tree and fell into the rain-pools beneath.

For Jimbo's state of oblivion in the tree was in reality a momentary return to consciousness in his body on the bed, and the repaired mechanism of the brain and muscles had summoned him back on a sort of trial visit. He remembered nothing of it afterwards, any more than one remembers the experiences of deep sleep; but the fact was that, with the descent of the darkness upon him in the branches, he had opened his eyes once again on the scene in the night-nursery bedroom where his body lay.

He saw figures standing round the bed and about the room; his mother with the same white face as before, was still bending over the bed asking him if he knew her; a tall man in a long black coat moved noiselessly to and fro; and he saw a shaded lamp on a table a little to the right of the bed. Nothing seemed to have changed very much, though there had probably been time enough since he last opened his eyes for the black-coated doctor to have gone and come again for a second visit. He held an instrument in his hands that shone brightly in the lamplight. Jimbo saw this plainly and wondered what it was. He felt as if he were just waking out of a nice, deep sleep—dreamless and undisturbed. The Empty House, the Governess, Fright and the Children had all vanished from his memory, and he knew no more about wings and feathers than he did about the science of meteorology.

But the bedroom scene was a mere glimpse after all; his eyes were already beginning to close again. First they shut out the figure of the doctor; then the bed-curtains; and then the nurse moved her arm, making the whole scene quiver for an instant, like some huge jelly-shape, before it dipped into profound darkness and disappeared altogether. His mother's voice ran off into a thin trickle of sound, miles and miles away, and the light from the lamp followed him with its glare for less than half a second. All had vanished.

ALGERNON BLACKWOOD

"Jimbo, dear, where have you been? Can you remember anything?" asked the soft voice beside him, as he looked first at the stars overhead, and then from the tracery of branches and leaves beneath him to the great sea of tree-tops and open country all round.

But he could tell her nothing; he seemed dreamy and absent-minded, lying and staring at her as if he hardly knew who she was or what she was saying. His mind was still hovering near the border-line of the two states of consciousness, like the region between sleeping and waking, where both worlds seem unreal and wholly wonderful.

He could not answer her questions, but he evidently caught some reflex of her emotions, for he leaned towards her across the branches, and said he was happy and never wanted to leave her. Then he crawled to the end of the big bough and sprang out into the air with a shout of delight. He was the child again—the flying child, wild with the excitement of tearing through the night air at fifty miles an hour.

The governess soon followed him and they flew home together, taking a long turn by the sea and past the great chalk cliffs, where the sea sang loud beneath them.

These lapses became with time more frequent, as well as of longer duration; and with them the boy noticed that the longing to escape became once again intense. He wanted *to get home*, wherever home was; he experienced a sort of nostalgia for the body, though he could not remember where that body lay. But when he asked the governess what this feeling meant, she only mystified him by her answers, saying that every one, in the body or out of it, felt a deep longing for their final *home*, though they might not have the least idea where it lay, or even to be able to recognise, much less to label, their longing.

His normal feelings, too, were slowly returning to him. The Older Self became more and more submerged. As he approached the state of ordinary, superficial consciousness, the characteristics of that state reflected themselves more and more in his thoughts and feelings. His memory still remained a complete blank; but he somehow felt that the things, places, and people he wanted to remember, had moved much nearer to him than before. Every day brought them more within his reach.

"All these forgotten things will come back to me soon, I know," he said one day to the governess, "and then I'll tell you all about them."

"Perhaps you'll remember me too then," she answered, a shadow passing across her face.

Jimbo clapped his hands with delight.

"Oh," he cried, "I should like to remember you, because that would make you a sort of two-people governess, and I should love you twice as much."

But with the gradual return to former conditions the feelings of age and experience grew dim and indefinite, his knowledge lessened, becoming obscure and confused, showing itself only in vague impressions and impulses, until at last it became quite the exception for the child-consciousness to be broken through by flashes of intuition and inspiration from the more deeply hidden memories.

For one thing, the deep horror of the Empty House and its owner now returned to him with full force. Fear settled down again over the room, and lurked in the shadows over the yard. A vivid dread seized him of the *other door* in the room—the door through which the Frightened Children had disappeared, but which had never opened since. It gradually became for him a personality in the room, a staring, silent, listening thing, always watching, always waiting. One day it would open and he would be caught! In a dozen ways like this the horror of the house entered his heart and made him long for escape with all the force of his being.

But the governess, too, seemed changing; she was becoming more vague and more mysterious. Her face was always sad now, and her eyes wistful; her manner became restless and uneasy, and in many little ways the child could not fail to notice that her mind was intent upon other things. He begged her to name the day for the final flight, but she always seemed to have some good excuse for putting it off.

"I feel frightened when you don't tell me what's going on," he said to her.

"It's the preparations for the last flight," she answered, "the flight of escape. He'll try to prevent us going together so that you should get lost. But it's better you shouldn't know too much," she added. "Trust me and have patience."

"Oh, that's what you're so afraid of," he said, "*separation*!" He was very proud indeed of the long word, and said it over several times to himself.

And the governess, looking out of the window at the fading sunlight, repeated to herself more than to him the word he was so proud of.

"Yes, that's what I'm so afraid of—separation; but if it means your salvation—" and her sentence remained unfinished as her eyes wandered far above the tops of the trees into the shadows of the sky.

ALGERNON BLACKWOOD

And Jimbo, drawn by the sadness of her voice, turned towards the window and noticed to his utter amazement that he could *see right through her*. He could see the branches of the trees *beyond* her body.

But the next instant she turned and was no longer transparent, and before the boy could say a word, she crossed the floor and disappeared from the room.

XVI

PREPARATION

Now that he was preparing to leave it, Jimbo began to realise more fully how things in this world of delirium—so the governess sometimes called it—were all terribly out of order and confused. So long as he was wholly in it and of it, everything had seemed all right; but, as he approached his normal condition again, the disorder became more and more apparent.

And the next few hours brought it home with startling clearness, and increased to fever heat the desire for final escape.

It was not so much a nonsense-world—it was too alarming for that—as a world of nightmare, wherein everything was distorted. Events in it were all out of proportion; effects no longer sprang from adequate causes; things happened in a dislocated sort of way, and there was no sequence in the order of their happening. Tiny occurrences filled him with disproportionate, inconceivable horror; and great events, on the other hand, passed him scathless. The spirit of disorder—monstrous, uncouth, terrifying—reigned supreme; and Jimbo's whole desire, though inarticulate, was to escape back into order and harmony again.

In contrast to all this dreadful uncertainty, the conduct of the governess stood out alone as the one thing he could count upon: she was sure and unfailing; he felt absolute confidence in her plans for his safety, and when he thought of her his mind was at rest. Come what might, she would always be there in time to help. The adventure over the sea had proved that; but, childlike, he thought chiefly of his own safety, and had ceased to care very much whether she escaped with him or not. It was the older Jimbo that preferred captivity to escape without her, whereas every minute now he was sinking deeper into the normal child state in which the intuitive flashes from the buried soul became more and more rare.

Meanwhile, there was preparation going on, secret and mysterious. He could feel it. Some one else besides the governess was making plans, and the boy began to dread the moment of escape almost as much as he desired it. The alternative appalled him—to live for ever in the horror

ALGERNON BLACKWOOD

of this house, bounded by the narrow yard, watched by Fright listening ever at his elbow, and visited by the horrible Frightened Children. Even the governess herself began to inspire him with something akin to fear, as her personality grew more and more mysterious. He thought of her as she stood by the window, with the branches of the tree visible through her body, and the thought filled him with a dreadful and haunting distress.

But this was only when she was absent; the moment she came into the room, and he looked into her kind eyes, the old feeling of security returned, and he felt safe and happy.

Once, during the day, she came up to see him, and this time with final instructions. Jimbo listened with rapt attention.

"Tonight, or tomorrow night we start," she said in a quiet voice. "You must wait till you hear me calling—"

"But sha'n't we start together?" he interrupted.

"Not exactly," she replied. "I'm doing everything possible to put him off the scent, but it's not easy, for once Fright knows you he's always on the watch. Even if he can't prevent your escape, he'll try to send you home to your body with such a shock that you'll be only 'half there' for the rest of your life."

Jimbo did not quite understand what she meant by this, and returned at once to the main point.

"Then the moment you call I'm to start?"

"Yes. I shall be outside somewhere. It depends on the wind and weather a little, but probably I shall be hovering above the trees. You must dash out of the window and join me the moment you hear me call. Clear the wall without sinking into the yard, and mind he doesn't tear your wings off as you fly by."

"What will happen, though, if I don't find you?" he asked.

"You might get lost. If he succeeds in getting me out of the way first, you're sure to get lost—"

"But I've had long flights without getting lost," he objected.

"Nothing to this one," she replied. "It will be tremendous. You see, Jimbo, it's not only distance; it's change of condition as well."

"I don't mind what it is so long as we escape together," he said, puzzled by her words.

He kept his eyes fixed on her face. It seemed to him she was changing even as he looked at her. A sort of veil lifted from her features. He fancied he could see the shape of the door through her body.

"Oh, please, Miss Lake—" he began in a frightened voice, taking a step towards her. "What is the matter? You look so different!"

"Nothing, dearest boy, is the matter," she replied faintly. "I feel sad at the thought of your—of our going, that's all. But that's nothing," she added more briskly, "and remember, I've told you exactly what to do; so you can't make any mistake. Now good-bye for the present."

There was a smile on her face that he had never seen there before, and an expression of tenderness and love that he could not fail to understand. But even as he looked she seemed to fade away into a delicate, thin shadow as she moved slowly towards the trap-door. Jimbo stretched out his arms to touch her, for the moment of dread had passed, and he wanted to kiss her.

"No!" she cried sharply. "Don't touch me, child; don't touch me!"

But he was already close beside her, and in another second would have had his arms round her, when his foot stumbled over something, and he fell forward into her with his full weight. Instead of saving himself against her body, however, he fell *clean through her*! Nothing stopped him; there was no resistance; he met nothing more solid than air, and fell full length upon the floor. Before he could recover from his surprise and pick himself up, something touched him on the lips, and he heard a voice that was faint as a whisper saying, "Good-bye, darling child, and bless you." The next moment he was on his feet again and the room was empty. The governess had gone through the trap-door, and he was alone.

It was all very strange and confusing, and he could not understand what was happening to her. He never for a moment realised that the change was in himself, and that as the tie between himself and his body became closer, the things of this other world he had been living in for so long must fade gradually away into shadows and emptiness.

But Jimbo was a brave boy; there was nothing of the coward in him, though his sensitive temperament made him sometimes hesitate where an ordinary child with less imagination would have acted promptly. The desire to cry he thrust down and repressed, fighting his depression by the thought that within a few hours the voice might sound that should call him to the excitement of the last flight—and freedom.

The rest of the daylight slipped away very quickly, and the room was full of shadows almost before he knew it. Then came the darkness. Outside, the wind rose and fell fitfully, booming in the chimney with hollow music, and sighing round the walls of the house. A few stars peeped between the branches of the elms, but masses of cloud hid most of the sky, and the air felt heavy with coming rain.

He lay down on the bed and waited. At the least sound he started, thinking it might be the call from the governess. But the few sounds he did hear always resolved themselves into the moaning of the wind, and no voice came. With his eyes on the open window, trying to pierce the gloom and find the stars, he lay motionless for hours, while the night wore on and the shadows deepened.

And during those long hours of darkness and silence he was conscious that a change was going on within him. Name it he could not, but somehow it made him feel that living people like himself were standing near, trying to speak, beckoning, anxious to bring him back into their own particular world. The darkness was so great that he could see only the square outline of the open window, but he felt sure that any sudden flash of light would have revealed a group of persons round his bed with arms outstretched, trying to reach him. The emotion they roused in him was not fear, for he felt sure they were kind, and eager only to help him; and the more he realised their presence, the less he thought about the governess who had been doing so much to make his escape possible.

Then, too, voices began to sound somewhere in the air, but he could not tell whether they were actually in the room, or outside in the night, or only within himself—in his own head:—strange, faint voices, whispering, laughing, shouting, crying; fragments of stories, rhymes, riddles, odd names of people and places jostled one another with varying degrees of clearness, now loud, now soft, till he wondered what it all meant, and longed for the light to come.

But besides all this, something else, too, was abroad that night— something he could not name or even think about without shaking with terror down at the very roots of his being. And when he thought of this, his heart called loudly for the governess, and the people hidden in the shadows of the room seemed quite useless and unable to help.

Thus he hovered between the two worlds and the two memories, phantoms and realities shifting and changing places every few minutes.

A little light would have saved him much suffering. If only the moon were up! Moonlight would have made all the difference. Even a moon half hidden and misty would have put the shadows farther away from him.

"Dear old misty moon!" he cried half aloud to himself upon the bed, "why aren't you here tonight? My last night!"

Misty Moon, Misty Moon! The words kept ringing in his head. Misty Moon, Misty Moon! They swam round in his blood in an odd, tumultuous rhythm. Every time the current of blood passed through his brain in the course of its circulation it brought the words with it, altered a little, and singing like a voice.

Like a voice! Suddenly he made the discovery that it actually *was* a voice—and not his own. It was no longer the blood singing in his veins, it was some one singing outside the window. The sound began faintly and far away, up above the trees; then it came gradually nearer, only to die away again almost to a whisper.

If it was not the voice of the governess, he could only say it was a very good imitation of it.

The words forming out of the empty air rose and fell with the wind, and, taking his thoughts, flung them in a stream through the dark sky towards the hidden, misty moon:

> *"O misty moon,*
> *Dear, misty moon,*
> *The nights are long without thee;*
> *The shadows creep*
> *Across my sleep,*
> *And fold their wings about me!"*

And another silvery voice, that might have been the voice of a star, took it up faintly, evidently from a much greater distance:

> *"O misty moon,*
> *Sweet, misty moon,*
> *The stars are dim behind thee;*
> *And, lo, thy beams*
> *Spin through my dreams*
> *And weave a veil to blind me!"*

The sound of this beautiful voice so delighted Jimbo that he sprang from his bed and rushed to the window, hoping that he might be able to hear it more clearly. But, before he got half-way across the room, he stopped short, trembling with terror. Underneath his very feet, in the depths of the house, he heard the awful voice he dreaded more than anything else. It roared out the lines with a sound like the rushing of a great river:

> *"O misty moon,*
> *Pale misty moon,*
> *Thy songs are nightly driven,*
> *Eternally,*
> *From sky to sky,*
> *O'er the old, grey Hills of Heaven!"*

And after the verse Jimbo heard a great peal of laughter that seemed to shake the walls of the house, and rooted his feet to the floor. It rolled away with thundering echoes into the very bowels of the earth. He just managed to crawl back to his mattress and lie down, when another voice took up the song, but this time in accents so tender, that the child felt something within him melt into tears of joy, and he was on the verge of recognising, for the first time since his accident, the voice of his mother:

> *"O misty moon,*
> *Shy, misty moon,*
> *Whence comes the blush that trembles*
> *In sweet disgrace*
> *O'er half thy face*
> *When Night her stars assembles?"*

But his memory, of course, failed him just as he seemed about to grasp it, and he was left wondering why the sound of that one voice had brought him a moment of radiant happiness in the midst of so much horror and pain. Meanwhile the answering voices went on, each time different, and in new directions.

But the next verse somehow brought back to him all the terror he had felt in his flight over the sea, when the sound of the hissing waters had reached his ears through the carpet of fog:

> *"O misty moon,*
> *Persuasive moon,*
> *Earth's tides are ever rising;*

By the awful grace
Of thy weird white face
Leap the seas to thy enticing!"

Then followed the voice that had started the horrid song. This time he was sure it was not Miss Lake's voice, but only a very clever imitation of it. Moreover, it again ended in a shriek of laughter that froze his blood:

"O misty moon,
Deceiving moon,
Thy silvery glance brings sadness;
Who flies to thee,
From land or sea,
Shall end—his—days—in—MADNESS!"

Other voices began to laugh and sing, but Jimbo stopped his ears, for he simply could not bear any more. He felt certain, too, that these strange words to the moon had all been part of a trap—a device to draw him to the window. He shuddered to think how nearly he had fallen into it, and determined to lie on the bed and wait till he heard his companion calling, and knew beyond all doubt that it was she.

But the night passed away and the dawn came, and no voice had called him forth to the last flight.

Hitherto, in all his experiences, there had been only one absolute certainty: the appearance of the governess with the morning light. But this time sunrise came and the clouds cleared away, and the sweet smells of field and air stole into the little room, yet without any sign of the governess. The hours passed, and she did not come, till finally he realised that she was not coming at all, and he would have to spend the whole day alone. Something had happened to prevent her, or else it was all part of her mysterious "plan." He did not know, and all he could do was to wait, and wonder, and hope.

All day long he lay and waited, and all day long he was alone. The trap-door never once moved; the courtyard remained empty and deserted; there was no sound on the landing or on the stairs; no wind stirred the leaves outside, and the hot sun poured down out of a cloudless sky. He stood by the open window for hours watching the motionless branches. Everything seemed dead; not even a bird crossed his field of vision. The loneliness, the awful silence, and above all, the dread of the approaching night, were sometimes more than he seemed able to bear; and he wanted to put his head out of the window and scream, or lie down on the bed and cry his heart out. But he yielded to neither impulse; he kept a brave heart, knowing that this would be his last night in prison, and that in a few hours' time he would hear his name called out of the sky, and would dash through the window to liberty and the last wild flight. This thought gave him courage, and he kept all his energy for the great effort.

Gradually, once more, the sunlight faded, and the darkness began to creep over the land. Never before had the shadows under the elms looked so fantastic, nor the bushes in the field beyond assumed such sinister shapes. The Empty House was being gradually invested; the enemy was masquerading already under cover of these very shadows.

Very soon, he felt, the attack would begin, and he must be ready to act.

The night came down at last with a strange suddenness, and with it the warning of the governess came back to him; he thought quakingly of the stricken children who had been caught and deprived of their wings; and then he pulled out his long red feathers and tried their strength, and gained thus fresh confidence in their power to save him when the time came.

XVII

OFF!

With the full darkness a whole army of horrors crept nearer. He felt sure of this, though he could actually see nothing. The house was surrounded, the courtyard crowded. Outside, on the stairs, in the other rooms, even on the roof itself, waited dreadful things ready to catch him, to tear off his wings, to make him prisoner for ever and ever.

The possibility that something had happened to the governess now became a probability. Imperceptibly the change was wrought; he could not say how or when exactly; but he now felt almost certain that the effort to keep her out of the way had succeeded. If this were true, the boy's only hope lay in his wings, and he pulled them out to their full length and kissed them passionately, speaking to the strong red feathers as if they were living little persons.

"You must save me! You will save me, won't you?" he cried in his anguish. And every time he did this and looked at them he gained fresh hope and courage.

The problem *where he was to fly to* had not yet insisted on a solution, though it lay always at the back of his mind; for the final flight of escape without a guide had never been even a possibility before.

Lying there alone in the darkness, waiting for the sound of the voice so longed-for, he found his thoughts turning again to the moon, and the strange words of the song that had puzzled him the night before. What in the world did it all mean? Why all this about the moon? Why was it a cruel moon, and why should it attract and persuade and entice him? He felt sure, the more he thought of it, that this had all been a device to draw him to the window—and perhaps even farther.

The darkness began to terrify him; he dreaded more and more the waiting, listening things that it concealed. Oh, when would the governess call to him? When would he be able to dash through the open window and join her in the sky?

He thought of the sunlight that had flooded the yard all day—so bright it seemed to have come from a sun fresh made and shining for the first time. He thought of the exquisite flowers that grew in the fields just beyond the high wall, and the night smells of the earth

ALGERNON BLACKWOOD

reached him through the window, wafted in upon a wind heavy with secrets of woods and fields. They all came from a Land of Magic that after tonight might be for ever beyond his reach, and they went straight to his heart and immediately turned something solid there into tears. But the tears did not find their natural expression, and Jimbo lay there fighting with his pain, keeping all his strength for the one great effort, and waiting for the voice that at any minute now might sound above the tree-tops.

But the hours passed and the voice did not come.

How he loathed the room and everything in it. The ceiling stretched like a white, staring countenance above him; the walls watched and listened; and even the mantelpiece grew into the semblance of a creature with drawn-up shoulders bending over him. The whole room, indeed, seemed to his frightened soul to run into the shape of a monstrous person whose arms were outstretched in all directions to prevent his escape.

His hands never left his wings now. He stroked and fondled them, arranging the feathers smoothly and speaking to them under his breath just as though they were living things. To him they were indeed alive, and he knew when the time came they would not fail him. The fierce passion for the open spaces took possession of his soul, and his whole being began to cry out for freedom, rushing wind, the stars, and a pathless sky.

Slowly the power of the great, open Night entered his heart, bringing with it a courage that enabled him to keep the terrors of the House at a distance.

So far, the boy's strength had been equal to the task, but a moment was approaching when the tension would be too great to bear, and the long pent-up force would rush forth into an act. Jimbo realised this quite clearly; though he could not exactly express it in words, he felt that his real hope of escape lay in the success of that act. Meanwhile, with more than a child's wisdom, he stored up every particle of strength he had for the great moment when it should come.

A light wind had risen soon after sunset, but as the night wore on it began to fail, dropping away into little silences that grew each time longer. In the heart of one of these spells of silence Jimbo presently noticed a new sound—a sound that he recognised.

Far away at first, but growing in distinctness with every dropping of the wind, this new sound rose from the interior of the house below and came gradually upon him. It was voices faintly singing, and the tread of stealthy footsteps.

Nearer and nearer came the sound, till at length they reached the door, and there passed into the room a wave of fine, gentle sound that woke no echo and scarcely seemed to stir the air into vibration at all. The door had opened, and a number of voices were singing softly under their breath.

And after the sounds, creeping slowly like some timid animal, there came into the room a small black figure just visible in the faint starlight. It peered round the edge of the door, hesitated a moment, and then advanced with an odd rhythmical sort of motion. And after the first figure came a second, and after the second a third; and then several entered together, till a whole group of them stood on the floor between Jimbo and the open window.

Then he recognised the Frightened Children and his heart sank. Even they, he saw, were arrayed against him, and took it for granted that he already belonged to them.

Oh, why did not the governess come for him? Why was there no voice in the sky? He glanced with longing towards the heavens, and as the children moved past, he was almost certain that he saw the stars *through* their bodies too.

Slowly they shuffled across the floor till they formed a semicircle round the bed; and then they began a silent, impish dance that made the flesh creep. Their thin forms were dressed in black gowns like shrouds, and as they moved through the steps of the bizarre measure he saw that their legs were little more than mere skin and bone. Their faces—what he could see of them when he dared to open his eyes—were pale as ashes, and their beady little eyes shone like the facets of cut stones, flashing in all directions. And while they danced in and out amongst each other, never breaking the semicircle round the bed, they sang a low, mournful song that sounded like the wind whispering through a leafless wood.

And the words stirred in him that vague yet terrible fear known to all children who have been frightened and made to feel afraid of the dark. Evidently his sensations were being merged very rapidly now into those of the little boy in the night-nursery bed.

> *"There is Someone in the Nursery*
> *Whom we never saw before;*
> *—Why hangs the moon so red?—*
> *And he came not by the passage,*

ALGERNON BLACKWOOD

Or the window, or the door;
—Why hangs the moon so red?—
And he stands there in the darkness,
In the centre of the floor.
—See, where the moon hangs red!—

Someone's hiding in the passage
Where the door begins to swing;
—Why drive the clouds so fast?—
In the corner by the staircase
There's a dreadful waiting thing:
—Why drive the clouds so fast?—
Past the curtain creeps a monster
With a black and fluttering wing;
—See, where the clouds drive fast!—

In the chilly dusk of evening;
In the hush before the dawn;
—Why drips the rain so cold?—
In the twilight of the garden,
In the mist upon the lawn,
—Why drips the rain so cold?—
Faces stare, and mouth upon us,
Faces white and weird and drawn;
—See, how the rain drips cold!—

Close beside us in the night-time,
Waiting for us in the gloom,
—O! Why sings the wind so shrill?—
In the shadows by the cupboard,
In the corners of the room,
—O! Why sings the wind so shrill?—
From the corridors and landings
Voices call us to our doom.
—O! how the wind sings shrill!"—

By this time the dreadful dancers had come much closer to him, shifting stealthily nearer to the bed under cover of their dancing, and always *between him and the window*.

Suddenly their intention flashed upon him; they meant to prevent his escape!

With a tremendous effort he sprang from the bed. As he did so a dozen pairs of thin, shadowy arms shot out towards him as though to seize his wings; but with an agility born of fright he dodged them, and ran swiftly into the corner by the mantelpiece. Standing with his back against the wall he faced the children, and strove to call out for help to the governess; but this time there was an entirely new difficulty in the way, for he found to his utter dismay that his voice refused to make itself heard. His mouth was dry and his tongue would hardly stir.

Not a sound issued from his lips, but the children instantly moved forwards and hemmed him in between them and the wall; and to reach the window he would have to break through this semicircle of whispering, shadowy forms. Above their heads he could see the stars shining, and any moment he might hear Miss Lake's voice calling to him to come out. His heart rose with passionate longing within him, and he gathered his wings tightly about him ready for the final dash. It would take more than the Frightened Children to hold him prisoner when once he heard that voice, or even without it!

Whether they were astonished at his boldness, or merely waiting their opportunity later, he could not tell; but anyhow they kept their distance for a time and made no further attempt to seize his feathers. Whispering together under their breath, sometimes singing their mournful, sighing songs, sometimes sinking their voices to a confused murmur, they moved in and out amongst each other with soundless feet like the shadows of branches swaying in the wind.

Then, suddenly, they moved closer and stretched out their arms towards him, their bodies swaying rhythmically together, while their combined voices, raised just above a whisper, sang to him—

> *"Dare you fly out tonight,*
> *When the Moon is so strong?*
> *Though the stars are so bright,*
> *There is death in their song;*
> *You're a hostage to Fright,*
> *And to us you belong!*
>
> *Dare you fly out alone*
> *Through the shadows that wave,*

　　　　　　　　　　　　　　ALGERNON BLACKWOOD

> *When the course is unknown*
> *And there's no one to save?*
> *You are bone of our bone,*
> *And for ever His slave!"*

And, following these words, came from somewhere in the air that voice like the thunder of a river. Jimbo knew only too well to whom it belonged as he listened to the rhyme of the West Wind—

> *"For the Wind of the West*
> *Is a wind unblest,*
> *And its dangerous breath*
> *Will entice you to death!*
> *Fly not with the Wind of the West, O child,*
> *With the terrible Wind of the West!"*

But the boy knew perfectly well that these efforts to stop him were all part of a trap. They were lying to him. It was not the Wind of the West at all; *it was the South Wind!* That at least he knew by the odours that were wafted in through the window. Again he tried to call to the governess, but his tongue lay stiff in his mouth and no sound came.

Meanwhile the children began to draw closer, hemming him in. They moved almost imperceptibly, but he saw plainly that the circle was growing smaller and smaller. His legs began to tremble, and he felt that soon he would collapse and drop at their feet, for his strength was failing and the power to act and move was slowly leaving him.

The little shadowy figures were almost touching him, when suddenly a new sound broke the stillness and set every nerve tingling in his body.

Something was shuffling along the landing. He heard it outside, pushing against the door. The handle turned with a rattle, and a moment later the door slowly opened.

For a second Jimbo's breath failed him, and he nearly fell in a heap upon the floor. Round the edge of the door he saw a dim huge figure come crawling into the room—creeping along the floor—and trailing behind it a pair of immense black wings that stretched along the boards. For one brief second he stared, horror-stricken, and wondering what it was. But before the whole length of the creature was in, he knew. It was Fright himself! *And he was making steadily for the window!*

The shock instantly galvanised the boy into a state of activity again. He recovered the use of all his muscles and all his faculties. His voice, released by terror, rang out in a wild shriek for help to the governess, and he dashed forward across the room in a mad rush for the window. Unless he could reach it before the other, he would be a prisoner for the rest of his life. It was now or never.

The instant he moved, the children came straight at him with hands outstretched to stop him; but he passed through them as if they were smoke, and with almost a single bound sprang upon the narrow window-sill. To do this he had to clear the head and shoulders of the creature on the floor, and though he accomplished it successfully, he felt himself clutched from behind. For a second he balanced doubtfully on the window ledge. He felt himself being pulled back into the room, and he combined all his forces into one tremendous effort to rush forward.

There was a ripping, tearing sound as he sprang into the air with a yell of mingled terror and exultation. His prompt action and the fierce impetus had saved him. He was free. But in the awful hand that seized him he had left behind the end feathers of his right wing. A few inches more and it would have been not merely the feathers, but the entire wing itself.

He dropped to within three feet of the stones in the yard, and then, borne aloft by the kind, rushing Wind of the South, he rose in a tremendous sweep far over the tops of the high elms and out into the heart of the night.

Only there was no governess's voice to guide him; and behind him, a little lower down, a black pursuing figure with huge wings flapped heavily as it followed with laborious flight through the darkness.

XVIII

Home

B ut it was the sound of something crashing heavily through the top branches of the elms that made the boy realise he was actually being followed; and all his efforts became concentrated into the desire to put as much distance as possible between himself and the horror of the Empty House.

He heard the noise of big wings far beneath him, and his one idea was to out-distance his pursuer and then come down again to earth and rest his wings in the branches of a tree till he could devise some plan how to find the governess. So at first he raced at full speed through the air, taking no thought of direction.

When he looked down, all he could see was that something vague and shadowy, shaking out a pair of enormous wings between him and the earth, move along with him. Its path was parallel with his own, but apparently it made no effort to rise up to his higher level. It thundered along far beneath him, and instinctively he raised his head and steered more and more upwards and away from the world.

The gap at the end of his right wing where the feathers had been torn out seemed to make no difference in his power of flight or steering, and he went tearing through the night at a pace he had never dared to try before, and at a height he had never yet reached in any of the practice flights. He soared higher even than he knew; and perhaps this was fortunate, for the friction of the lower atmosphere might have heated him to the point of igniting, and some watcher at one of earth's windows might have suddenly seen a brilliant little meteor flash through the night and vanish into dust.

At first the joy of escape was the only idea his mind seemed able to grasp; he revelled in a passionate sense of freedom, and all his energies poured themselves into one concentrated effort to fly faster, faster, faster. But after a time, when the pursuer had been apparently outflown, and he realised that escape was an accomplished fact, he began to search for the governess, calling to her, rising and falling, darting in all directions, and then hovering on outstretched wings to try and catch some sound of a friendly voice.

But no answer came, either from the stars that crowded the vault above, or from the dark surface of the world below; only silence answered his cries, and his voice was swallowed up and lost in the immensity of space almost the moment it left his lips.

Presently he began to realise to what an appalling distance he had risen above the world, and with anxious eyes he tried to pierce the gaping emptiness beneath him and on all sides. But this vast sea of air had nothing to reveal. The stars shone like pinholes of gold pricked in a deep black curtain; and the moon, now rising slowly, spread a veil of silver between him and the upper regions. There was not a cloud anywhere and the winds were all asleep. He was alone in space. Yet, as the swishing of his feathers slackened and the roar in his ears died away, he heard in the short pause the ominous beating of great wings somewhere in the depths beneath him, and knew that the great pursuer was still on his track.

The glare of the moon now made it impossible to distinguish anything properly, and in these huge spaces, with nothing to guide the eye, it was difficult to know exactly from what direction the sound came. He was only sure of one thing—that it was far below him, and that for the present it did not seem to come much nearer. The cry for help that kept rising to his lips he suppressed, for it would only have served to guide his pursuer; and, moreover, a cry—a little thin, despairing cry— was instantly lost in these great heavens. It was less than a drop in an ocean.

On and on he flew, always pointing away from the earth, and trying hard to think where he would find safety. Would this awful creature hunt him all night long into the daylight, or would he be forced back into the Empty House in sheer exhaustion? The thought gave him new impetus, and with powerful strokes he dashed onwards and upwards through the wilderness of space in which the only pathways were the little golden tracks of the starbeams. The governess would turn up somewhere; he was positive of that. She had never failed him yet.

So, alone and breathless, he pursued his flight, and the higher he went the more the tremendous vault opened up into inconceivable and untold distances. His speed kept increasing; he thought he had never found flying so easy before; and the thunder of the following wings that held persistently on his track made it dangerous for him to slacken up for more than a minute here and there. The earth became a dark blot beneath him, while the moon, rising higher and higher, grew weirdly bright and close. How black the sky was; how piercing the points of starlight; how stimulating the strong, new odours of these lofty regions! He realised with a thrill of genuine awe that he had flown over the very edge of the world, and the moment the thought entered his mind it was flung back at him by a voice that seemed close to his ear one moment, and the next was miles away in the space overhead. Light thoughts, born of the stars and the moon and of his great speed, danced before his mind in fanciful array. Once he laughed aloud at them, but once only. The sound of his voice in these echoless spaces made him afraid.

The speed, too, affected his vision, for at one moment thin clouds stretched across his face, and the next he was whirling through perfectly clear air again with no vestige of a cloud in sight. The same reason doubtless explained the sudden presence of sheets of light in the air that reflected the moonlight like particles of glittering ice, and then suddenly disappeared again. The terrific speed would explain a good many things, but certainly it was curious how creatures formed out of the hollow darkness, like foam before a steamer's bows, and moved noiselessly away on either side to join the army of dim life that crowded everywhere and watched his passage. For, in front and on both sides, there gathered a vast assembly of silent forms more than shadows, less than bodily shapes, that opened up a pathway as he rushed through them, and then immediately closed up their ranks again when he had passed. The air seemed packed with living creatures. Space was filled with them. They surrounded him on all sides. Yet his passage through them was like the passage of a hand through smoke; it was easy to make a pathway, but the pathway left no traces behind it. More smoke rushed in and filled the void.

He could never see these things properly, face to face; they always kept just out of the line of vision, like shadows that follow a lonely walker in a wood and vanish the moment he turns to look at them over his shoulder. But ever by his side, with a steady, effortless motion, he knew they kept up with him—strange inhabitants of the airless heights, immense and misty-winged, with veiled, flaming eyes and silent feathers. He was not afraid of them; for they were neither friendly nor hostile; they were simply the beings of another world, alien and unknown.

But what puzzled him more was that the light and the darkness seemed separate things, each distinctly visible. After each stroke of his wings he *saw the darkness* sift downwards past him through the air like dust. It floated all round him in thinnest diaphanous texture—visible, not because the moonlight made it so, but because in its inmost soul it was itself luminous. It rose and fell in eddies, swirling wreaths, and undulations; inwoven with starbeams, as with golden thread, it clothed him about in circles of some magical primordial substance.

Even the stars, looking down upon him from terrifying heights, seemed now draped, now undraped, as if by the sweeping of enormous wings that stirred these sheets of visible darkness into a vast system of circulation through the heavens. Everything in these oceans of upper space apparently made use of wings, or the idea of wings. Perhaps even the great earth itself, rolling from star to star, was moved by the power of gigantic, invisible wings! . . .

Jimbo realised he had entered a forbidden region. He began to feel afraid.

But the only possible expression of his fear, and its only possible relief, lay in his own wings—and he used them with redoubled energy. He dashed forward so fast that his face begun to burn, and he kept turning his head in every direction for a sign of the governess, or for some indication of where he could *escape to*. In the pauses of the wild flight he heard the thunder of the following wings below. They were still on his trail, and it seemed that they were gaining on him.

He took a new angle, realising that his only chance was to fly high; and the new course took him perpendicularly away from the earth and straight towards the moon. Later, when he had out-distanced the other creature, he would drop down again to safer levels.

Yet the hours passed and it never overtook him. A measured distance was steadily kept up between them as though with calculated purpose.

Curious distant voices shouted from time to time all manner of sentences and rhymes in his ears, but he could neither understand nor remember them. More and more the awful stillness of the vast regions that lie between the world and the moon appalled him.

Then, suddenly, a new sound reached him that at first he could not in the least understand. It reached him, however, not through the ears, but by a steady trembling of the whole surface of his body. It set him in vibration all over, and for some time he had no idea what it meant. The trembling ran deeper and deeper into his body, till at last a single, powerful, regular vibration took complete possession of his whole being, and he felt as though he was being wrapped round and absorbed by this vast and gigantic sound. He had always thought that the voice of Fright, like the roar of a river, was the loudest and deepest sound he had ever heard. Even that set his soul a-trembling. But this new, tremendous, rolling-ocean of a voice came not that way, and could not be compared to it. The voice of the other was a mere tickling of the ear compared to this awful crashing of seas and mountains and falling worlds. It must break him to pieces, he felt.

Suddenly he knew what it was,—and for a second his wings failed him:—he had reached such a height that he could hear the roar of the world as it thundered along its journey through space! That was the meaning of this voice of majesty that set him all a-trembling. And before long he would probably hear, too, the voices of the planets, and the singing of the great moon. The governess had warned him about this. At the first sound of these awful voices she told him to turn instantly and drop back to the earth as fast as ever he could drop.

Jimbo turned instinctively and began to fall. But, before he had dropped half a mile, he met once again the ascending sound of the wings that had followed him from the Empty House.

It was no good flying straight into destruction. He summoned all his courage and turned once more towards the stars. Anything was better than being caught and held for ever by Fright, and with a wild cry for help that fell dead in the empty spaces, he renewed his unending flight towards the stars.

But, meanwhile, the pursuer had distinctly gained. Appalled by the mighty thunder of the stars' voices above, and by the prospect of immediate capture if he turned back, Jimbo flew blindly on towards the moon, regardless of consequences. And below him the Pursuer came closer and closer. The strokes of its wings were no longer mere distant thuds that he heard when he paused in his own flight to listen; they were the audible swishing of feathers. It was near enough for that.

Jimbo could never properly see what was following him. A shadow between him and the earth was all he could distinguish, but in the centre of that shadow there seemed to burn two glowing eyes. Two brilliant lights flashed whenever he looked down, like the lamps of a revolving lighthouse. But other things he saw, too, when he looked down, and once the earth rose close to his face so that he could have touched it with his hands. The same instant it dropped away again with a rush of whirlwinds, and became a distant shadow miles and miles below him. But before it went, he had time to see the Empty House standing within its gloomy yard, and the horror of it gave him fresh impetus.

Another time when the world raced up close to his eyes he saw a scene of a different kind that stirred a passionately deep yearning within him—a house overgrown with ivy and standing among trees and gardens, with laburnums and lilacs flowering on smooth green lawns, and a clean gravel drive leading down to a big pair of iron gates. Oh, it all seemed so familiar! Perhaps in another minute the well-known figures would have appeared and spoken to him. Already he heard their voices behind the bushes. But, just before they appeared, the earth dropped back with a roar of a thousand winds, and Jimbo saw instead the shadow of the Pursuer mounting, mounting, mounting towards him. Up he shot again with terror in his heart, and all trembling with the thunder of the great star-voices above. He felt like a leaf in a hurricane, "lost, dizzy, shelterless."

Voices, too, now began to be heard more frequently. They dropped upon him out of the reaches of this endless void; and with them sometimes came forms that shot past him with amazing swiftness, racing into the empty Beyond as though sucked into a vast vacuum. The very stars seemed to move. He became part of some much larger movement in which he was engulfed and merged. He could no longer think of himself as Jimbo. When he uttered his own name he saw merely a mass of wind and colour through which the great pulses of space and the planets beat tumultuously, lapping him round with the currents of a terrific motion that seemed to swallow up his own little personality entirely, while giving him something infinitely greater. . .

But surely these small voices, shrill and trumpet-like, did not come from the stars! these deep whispers that ran round the immense vault overhead and sounded almost familiarly in his ears—

"Give it him the moment he wakes."

"Bring the ice-bag. . . quick!"

"Put the hot bottle to his feet IMMEDIATELY!"

The voices shrieked all round him, turning suddenly into soft whispers that died away somewhere among his feathers. The soles of his feet began to glow, and he felt a gigantic hand laid upon his throat and head. Almost it seemed as if he were lying somewhere on his back, and people were bending over him, shouting and whispering.

"Why hangs the moon so red?" cried a voice that was instantly drowned in a chorus of unintelligible whispering.

ALGERNON BLACKWOOD

"The black cow must be killed," whispered some one deep within the sky.

"Why drips the rain so cold?" yelled one of the hideous children close behind him. And a third called with a distant laughter from behind a star—

"Why sings the wind so shrill?"

"QUIET!" roared an appalling voice below, as if all the rivers of the world had suddenly turned loose into the sky. "QUIET!"

Instantly a star, that had been hovering for some time on the edge of a fantastic dance, dropped down close in front of his face. It had a glaring disc, with mouth and eyes. An icy hand seemed laid on his head, and the star rushed back into its place in the sky, leaving a trail of red flame behind it. A little voice seemed to go with it, growing fainter and fainter in the distance—

"We dance with phantoms and with shadows play."

But, regardless of everything, Jimbo flew onwards and upwards, terrified and helpless though he was. His thoughts turned without ceasing to the governess, and he felt sure that she would yet turn up in time to save him from being caught by the Fright that pursued, or lost among the fearful spaces that lay beyond the stars.

For a long time, however, his wings had been growing more and more tired, and the prospect of being destroyed from sheer exhaustion now presented itself to the boy vaguely as a possible alternative—vaguely only, because he was no longer able to think, properly speaking, and things came to him more by way of dull feeling than anything else.

It was all the more with something of a positive shock, therefore, that he realised the change. For a change had come. He was now sudden by conscious of an influx of new power—greater than anything he had ever known before in any of his flights. His wings now suddenly worked as if by magic. Never had the motion been so easy, and it became every minute easier and easier. He simply flashed along without apparent effort. An immense driving power had entered into him. He realised that he could fly for ever without getting tired. His pace increased tenfold—increased alarmingly. The possibility of exhaustion vanished utterly. Jimbo knew now that something was wrong. This new driving power was something wholly outside himself. His wings were working far too easily. Then, suddenly, he understood: *His wings were not working at all!*

He was not being driven forward from behind; he was being drawn forward from in front.

He saw it all in a flash: Miss Lake's warning long ago about the danger of flying too high; the last song of the Frightened Children, "Dare you fly out alone through the shadows that wave, when the course is unknown and there's no one to save?" the strange words sung to him about the "relentless misty moon," and the object of the dreadful Pursuer in steadily forcing him upwards and away from the earth. It all flashed across his poor little dazed mind. He understood at last.

He had soared too high and had entered the sphere of the moon's attraction.

"The moon is too strong, and there's death in the stars!" a voice bellowed below him like the roar of a falling mountain, shaking the sky.

The child flew screaming on. There was nothing else he could do. But hardly had the roar died away when another voice was heard, a tender voice, a whispering, sympathetic voice, though from what part of the sky it came he could not tell—

"Arrange the pillows for his little head."

But below him the wings of the Pursuer were mounting closer and closer. He could almost feel the mighty wind from their feathers, and hear the rush of the great body between them. It was impossible to slacken his speed even had he wished; no strength on earth could have resisted that terrible power drawing upwards towards the moon. Instinctively, however, he realised that he would rather have gone forwards than backwards. He never could have faced capture by that dreadful creature behind. All the efforts of the past weeks to escape from Fright, the owner of the Empty House, now acted upon him with a cumulative effect, and added to the suction of the moon-life. He shot forward at a pace that increased with every second.

At the back of his mind, too, lay some kind of faint perception that the governess would, after all, be there to help him. She had always turned up before when he was in danger, and she would not fail him now. But this was a mere ghost of a thought that brought little comfort, and merely added its quota of force to the speed that whipped him on, ever faster, into the huge white moon-world in front.

For this, then, he had escaped from the horror of the Empty House! To be sucked up into the moon, the "relentless, misty moon"—to be drawn into its cruel, silver web, and destroyed. The Song to the Misty Moon outside the window came back in snatches and added to his

ALGERNON BLACKWOOD

terror; only it seemed now weeks ago since he had heard it. Something of its real meaning, too, filtered down into his heart, and he trembled anew to think that the moon could be a great, vast, moving Being, alive and with a purpose. . .

But why, oh, why did they keep shouting these horrid snatches of the song through the sky? Trapped! Trapped! The word haunted him through the night:

> *Thy songs are nightly driven,*
> *From sky to sky,*
> *Eternally,*
> *O'er the old, grey hills of heaven!*

Caught! Caught at last! The moon's prisoner, a captive in her airless caves; alone on her dead white plains; searching for ever in vain for the governess; wandering alone and terrified.

> *By the awful grace*
> *Of thy weird white face.*

The thought crazed him, and he struggled like a bird caught in a net. But he might as well have struggled to push the worlds out of their courses. The power against him was the power of the universe in which he was nothing but a little, lost, whirling atom. It was all of no avail, and the moon did not even smile at his feeble efforts. He was too light to revolve round her, too impalpable to create his own orbit; he had not even the consistency of a comet; he had reached the point of stagnation, as it were—the dead level—the neutral zone where the attractions of the earth and moon meet and counterbalance one another—where bodies have no weight and existence no meaning.

Now the moon was close upon him; he could see nothing else. There lay the vast, shining sea of light in front of him. Behind, the roar of the following creature grew fainter and fainter, as he outdistanced it in the awful swiftness of the huge drop down upon the moon mountains.

Already he was close enough to its surface to hear nothing of its great singing but a deep, confused murmur. And, as the distance increased, he realised that the change in his own condition increased. He felt as if he were flying off into a million tiny particles—breaking up under the effects of the deadly speed and the action of the new moon-forces.

Immense, invisible arms, half-silver and half-shadow, grew out of the white disc and drew him downwards upon her surface. He was being merged into the life of the moon.

There was a pause. For a moment his wings stopped dead. Their vain fluttering was all but over. . .

Hark! Was that a voice borne on the wings of some lost wind? Why should his heart beat so tumultuously all at once?

He turned and stared into the ocean of black air overhead till it turned him dizzy. A violent trembling ran through his tired being from head to foot. He had heard a voice—a voice that he knew and loved—a voice of help and deliverance. It rang in shrill syllables up the empty spaces, and it reached new centres of force within him that touched his last store of courage and strength.

"Jimbo, hold on!" it cried, like a faint, thin, pricking current of sound almost unable to reach him through the seas of distance. "I'm coming; hold on a little longer!"

It was the governess. She was true to the end. Jimbo felt his heart swell within him. She was mounting, mounting behind him with incredible swiftness. The sound of his own name in these terrible regions recalled to him some degree of concentration, and he strove hard to fight against the drawing power that was seeking his destruction.

He struggled frantically with his wings. But between him and the governess there was still the power of Fright to be overcome—the very Power she had long ago invoked. It was following him still, preventing his turning back, and driving him ever forward to his death.

Again the voice sounded in the night; and this time it was closer. He could not quite distinguish the words. They buzzed oddly in his ears. . . other voices mingled with them. . . the hideous children began to shriek somewhere underneath him. . . wings with eyes among their burning feathers flashed past him.

His own wings folded close over his little body, drooping like dead things. His eyes closed, and he turned on his side. A huge face that was one-half the governess and the other half the head gardener at home, thrust itself close against his own, and blew upon his eyelids till he opened them. Already he was falling, sinking, tumbling headlong through a space that offered no resistance.

"Jimbo!" shrieked a voice that instantly died away into a wail behind him.

He opened his eyes once more—for it was that loved voice again—

but the glare from the moon so dazzled him that he could only fancy he saw the figure of the governess, not a hundred feet away, struggling and floundering in the clutch of a black creature that beat the air with enormous wings all round her. He saw her hair streaming out into the night, and one wing seemed to hang broken and useless at her side.

He was turning over and over, like a piece of wood in the waves of the sea, and the governess, caught by Fright, the monster of her own creation, drifted away from his consciousness as a dream melts away in the light of the morning. . . From the gleaming mountains and treeless plains below Jimbo thought there rose a hollow roar like the mocking laughter of an immense multitude of people, shaking with mirth. The Moon had got him at last, and her laughter ran through the heavens like a wave. Revolving upon his own little axis so swiftly that he neither saw nor heard anything more, he dropped straight down upon the great satellite.

The light of the moon flamed up into his eyes and dazzled him.

But what in the world was this?

How could the moon dwindle so suddenly to the size of a mere lamp flame?

How could the whole expanse of the heavens shrink in an instant to the limits of a little, cramped room?

In a single second, before he had time to realise that he felt surprise, the entire memory of his recent experiences vanished from his mind. The past became an utter blank. Like a wreath of smoke everything melted away as if it had never been at all. The functions of the brain resumed their normal course. The delirium of the past few hours was over.

Jimbo was lying at home on his bed in the night-nursery, and his mother was bending over him. At the foot of the bed stood the doctor in black. The nurse held a lamp, only half shaded by her hand, as she approached the bedside.

This lamp was the moon of his delirium—only he had quite forgotten now that there had ever been any moon at all.

The little thermometer, thrust into his teeth among the stars, was still in his mouth. A hot-water bottle made his feet glow and burn. And from the walls of the sick-room came as it were the echoes of recently-uttered sentences: "Take his temperature! Give him the medicine the moment he wakes! Put the hot bottle to his feet. . . Fetch the ice-bag. . . Quick!"

"Where am I, mother?" he asked in a whisper.

"You're in bed, darling, and must keep quite quiet. You'll soon be all right again. It was the old black cow that tossed you. The gardener found you by the swinging gate and carried you in... You've been unconscious!"

"How long have I been uncon—?" Jimbo could not manage the whole word.

"About three hours, darling."

Then he fell into a deep, dreamless sleep, and when he woke long after it was early morning, and there was no one in the room but the old family nurse, who sat watching beside the bed. Something—some dim memory—that had stirred his brain in sleep, immediately rushed to his lips in the form of an inconsequent question. But before he could even frame the sentence, the thought that prompted it had slipped back into the deeper consciousness he had just left behind with the trance of deep sleep.

But the old nurse, watching every movement, waiting upon the child's very breath, had caught the question, and she answered soothingly in a whisper—

"Oh, Miss Lake died a few days after she left here," she said in a very low voice. "But don't think about her any more, dearie! She'll never frighten children again with her silly stories."

"*Died!*"

Jimbo sat up in bed and stared into the shadows behind her, as though his eyes saw something she could not see. But his voice seemed almost to belong to some one else.

"She was really dead all the time, then," he said below his breath.

Then the child fell back without another word, and dropped off into the sleep which was the first step to final recovery.

The End

bookfinity™

Discover more of your favorite classics with Bookfinity™.

- Track your reading with custom book lists.
- Get great book recommendations for your personalized Reader Type.
- Add reviews for your favorite books.
- AND MUCH MORE!

Visit **bookfinity.com** and take the fun Reader Type quiz to get started.

Enjoy our classic and modern companion pairings!

Printed in the USA
CPSIA information can be obtained
at www.ICGtesting.com
JSHW082356140824
68134JS00020B/2107

9 781513 283111